THE STORY OF US

SERENITY HOUSE BOOK ONE

MOLLY O'KEEFE

Copyright © 2018 by Molly Fader

All rights reserved.

No part of this book may be reproduced in any form or by any electronic or mechanical means, including information storage and retrieval systems, without written permission from the author, except for the use of brief quotations in a book review.

❦ Created with Vellum

SAMANTHA COULDN'T BREATHE

My son. Here.

What should I do? Say? What do I say to him?

The ceiling above her head creaked while J.D. moved around upstairs, and horror broke over her like a thunderstorm.

Oh, my God.

Her heart stopped dead cold in her chest.

The reality of the situation hammered her right in the stomach.

J.D.

Her son.

What were the chances that her son and J.D. would be here at the same time? What were the seriously cosmically screwed-up odds on that event?

After all these years, J.D. was finally going to learn her secret.

READER LETTER

Dear Reader,

A version of this book was published by Harlequin in 2008. It was a Superromance titled – The Son Between Them. Since getting the rights back, I've rewritten the story. I wanted to do a secret-baby book—but one with a twist. I also wanted to explore a long-standing relationship that was somehow both respectful and had no questions asked on both sides. How the mob got involved, I'm not too sure. But this book was a pleasure and an adventure to write. I wish all my heroes could be as intriguing as J.D. and all my heroines as rock solid as Sam.

The second book in this series is out now, too. Single Mom Jennifer and her son Spencer get their hard-earned HEA!

And Then There Was You

Please drop me a line at Molly@Molly-OKeefe.com to let me know what you think of J.D. and Sam. Or sign up for my newsletter!

I always love to hear from readers!
Happy reading,
Molly O'Keefe

1

The young ones, as a rule, were hard.

The young *pregnant* ones were heartbreaking.

Samantha Riggins watched the girl sitting in her office, clearly trying hard not to cry, and wondered how many more young pregnant girls Sam could help before jumping off the deep end.

There was a limit. There had to be.

"She hasn't said anything?" Samantha asked Deb, who'd checked in the girl while Sam taught an evening computer class.

"Nothing helpful," Deb said with a heavy sigh and arched eyebrows that reminded Sam that the young pregnant ones never said anything helpful. "Gave us the name Jane Doe and insisted she's twenty-one."

If Jane Doe was twenty-one Sam would eat her dog Daisy's dinner. "Anything else?" she asked, turning to watch Deb, who had walked in the doors of Serenity House Women's Shelter four years ago just like Jane Doe. Young. Pregnant. Terrified.

At least Jane Doe didn't appear beaten. Not like Deb had been, beaten to within an inch of dying.

"She's scared," Deb said, leaning against the kitchen counter. "But she's not talking. She's from the East Coast, maybe New York." She shook her head, her turquoise-and-rhinestone glasses catching the last of the light through the windows and tossing it around the room. "And that black hair is about as real as mine," Deb said, touching the blond tips of her long black braids. "She's got dye on her neck and hands. She's running, that girl, and she's not looking back."

Sam's worst suppositions were realized. Of course, young, pregnant women with bus-station dye jobs didn't show up at Serenity House because they'd heard the food was good.

They came because Northwoods, North Carolina, was the last stop on the southernmost tracks of a train heading out of the snarl that was New York, Newark, D.C. and Baltimore.

And they came because they were in trouble.

"For what it's worth, there's something about her that seems different," Deb said. "She's got a manicure. And a diamond ring she's wearing on a chain around her neck, that she ain't hocked yet. And them jeans she's got on cost two hundred dollars."

Sam shot Deb a dubious look. As if any of them would know two-hundred-dollar jeans if they came up and bit them in the butt.

"I read *People*," Deb explained. "They talk a lot about expensive jeans in that magazine. Can't help it if I've got an eye for fashion."

Sam smiled. Calling Deb's obsession with sequins and studding an "eye" was stretching it.

"All I'm saying is that girl is running from money," Deb said. "And that ain't ever a good thing for us."

No. It wasn't. It meant whomever this girl was running from had resources. Lawyers. Private investigators.

Luckily, Serenity House had a private investigator they could call, too, if they needed. But Sam was always careful about calling J.D.

"Thank you," she said to Deb, who, in the years since arriving and staying, had become the most valued asset Serenity House had. And not just because Deb's mother had taught her about plumbing.

"No problem," the young woman said and checked her watch. "It's eight o'clock. I need to pick up Shonny and get on home." She looked at Sam askance. "Unless you want me to stay here tonight?"

"No, thank you, Deb," Sam said, appreciating the offer. "We'll be okay."

"All right then, you want me to call J.D., get his help on this?"

The ripple that pulsed through her body was a familiar one. It happened anytime someone said his name.

"I'll call him after I talk to her," Sam said, making sure not to look at the shrewd Deb. Her secrets were under lock and key, but Deb was pretty good with locks, too.

Sam stepped into her cluttered office without looking at the girl who had gone rigid. While most people's offices were their sanctuary, Sam's was her garbage disposal. Her trash heap. Her storage closet. Her giant pounding headache. Books. Receipts. Sheets for the single beds, towels for the showers. Boxes of soap, all piled up around her desk.

And now amongst the clutter and flotsam was one thin, terrified, probably six-months-pregnant girl.

Just one more thing to wash up on her shores.

Sam made a big production of setting down her class notes, then cleaning stuff off her desk. Organizing files, throwing things out, all while watching the girl from under her eyelashes.

Oh, Jane Doe was scared. And Deb was right, the girl had cash. All the details pointed to money. She had good skin. Her face was full, as though she hadn't gone hungry a day in her life. No track marks on her arms. And, most telling, she had great teeth—sparkling white and straight. Dental hygiene, for the women who usually walked through the doors, was pretty far down the priority list.

Those teeth of Jane Doe's put Sam's instincts on full alert.

Sam had a responsibility to the rest of the women who used this shelter. While there were only two living here at the moment, they had all been brutalized in some fashion and they didn't need what this girl was running from to come hammering on the door in the wee hours of the morning.

"So," she finally said, studying her half-finished grocery list as though it was the girl's induction papers. "Jane."

The girl nodded, the flat black of her hair swallowing the light from the lamp on the desk. Dye job. All the way. "That's me," the girl said, her voice sounding as though it was dragged across sandpaper before coming out her lips.

"You want to tell me what's going on?" Sam asked. She sat back in her whiny chair and crossed her legs, careful to avoid the duct tape on the seat that snagged all of her tights. "What we can do to help you?"

"I just need a place to stay for a few nights," she said, the words tumbling out in a rush, as if she realized Sam might say no.

"We're not a hotel," Sam said. "And while I am happy to let you stay here tonight, I can only do so if you answer some questions."

"I already answered a bunch of questions," Jane said. "That other woman asked them."

"Well, I have a few more you need to answer."

"Or what?" she asked, the pale skin of her face practically vibrating, her whole body tuned to some high frequency. The edge of her Tommy Hilfiger T-shirt trembled, channeling the energy of the thin body beneath it.

"Or, perhaps you would be better helped by the police."

Jane swallowed and shook her head. "I can't go to the police."

"Why not?"

"Does it matter?" the girl asked, her blue eyes flashing. "My name is Jane. I'm twenty-one and my boyfriend hit me. I am scared for myself and my baby so you have to take me in."

Sam's eyebrows rose in surprise. "I don't, Jane. This is not a government facility. We are primarily privately funded. And as the executive director, I choose who we help and who I send on to the police. I have a responsibility to the women who live here." Not that there were that many. Jane was their only new resident in two months, but she didn't need to know that. "I have to keep them safe and if you can't tell me what I need to know, I will have to call the police."

They locked eyes, a showdown that Sam had been in and won too many times to count. But she had to give the girl credit, she was not going down without a fight.

"Jane." She sighed. "I want to help you. I spend my life helping women in your position. If you answer my questions, I can take better care of you. I am not the enemy."

Jane's lip trembled before she bit it so hard the pink skin

turned white. Sam held her breath and finally exhaled when Jane looked down at her hands, the battle over.

"What do you need to know?"

"Is there someone looking for you?"

Jane's throat bobbed. "He thinks I'm visiting my sister at school."

Sam didn't point out that sisters could be called. Cover stories could be blown.

"How old are you?" she asked.

"Twenty-one."

"Jane—"

Her blue eyes blazed. "I'm twenty-one and it was consensual and I want this baby. I want—" Tears flooded those eyes, dousing the fire. "I want this baby," she whispered. "I just need a few days to think."

There was no question Jane had lied about her age, but the rest of it smelled like the truth. The truth doused with the acrid tang of fear. Whatever this girl had behind her it wasn't good.

"Have you broken the law? Is that why you're running?"

Jane's brow furrowed as if she were thinking. "No," she finally answered. "I'm pretty sure I haven't broken any laws. I didn't steal anything. I didn't hurt anyone."

"Does your family—"

"They don't know anything," she snapped. "I made sure they don't know anything. My dad would—" Jane stopped, stared hard at her hands and didn't say another word.

"Your dad would what?" Sam asked carefully, feeling the tension in the air like humidity.

"Nothing," the girl said, not looking up from her hands. "My dad's got nothing to do with this."

The hair on the back of Sam's neck didn't like that answer one bit.

"It's late." Sam took pity on the poor girl. "I can give you a room for the night, but tomorrow morning you and I are going to have a talk."

"I'm telling the truth," Jane said, defensive and stoic. "I swear to you."

And if Sam had money for every time someone swore the truth to her, she would have retired to a tropical island long ago.

"Okay." Sam nodded. "For your protection and for the protection of the other women who live here I do have to notify the police. Chief Bigham will have a patrol car out front."

Jane's chin jerked. "You won't tell them—"

"Sweetheart, I don't know anything to tell them. But if someone has filed a missing person report on you, it's only a matter of time."

"I know." Jane's shoulders bent under an unseen weight.

Sam had learned the hard way over the years that, with the young pregnant ones, the person who filed the missing person report was often the threat. Mothers or fathers so angry with their child's mistakes that they lost their minds. Or boyfriends. They could lose their minds, too.

Serenity House could help Jane until the police came looking for her. Laws protected women's shelters.

Too bad they couldn't do as much for the young pregnant girls who could use the protection. She'd seen a lot of girls beaten down by the system, chewed up and spit right back out to the people who abused them and Sam wasn't sure how much justice there was in that.

"Let's get you to bed," Sam said, unlocking the top drawer of her old metal desk and grabbing the key to room three. "Things will seem better in the morning."

She led Jane Doe of the bad hair and fancy pants, from

her office right into the kitchen. Dinner had finished about an hour ago and the dishwasher chugged quietly in the evening shadows. The wooden counters, table and two high chairs were wiped clean and the smell of Deb's spaghetti lingered in the air.

"I thought a women's shelter would look different," Jane said.

"What do you mean?"

"This is like a house," the girl said, shrugging.

"I should hope so," Sam said, proud of the handsome two-story brick house with the stained-glass windows and the classroom addition built off the side. "It's my home."

"You live here?"

I rarely leave here, she thought, but only nodded.

"Is there air-conditioning?" Jane asked, pulling at the neck of her shirt. It was late June in North Carolina and the nights weren't cooling off the way they had a few weeks ago.

"Yes," she said. "We turn it off at night. Your room has a fan. Breakfast is at seven," she said. "On weekdays we serve breakfast to women and children in the community. But on the weekends it's just us. We take turns cooking and if you miss breakfast, there's nothing hot until dinner. But there's usually fruit and granola bars." Sam opened the big pantry cupboards and snagged two granola bars and handed them to Jane.

They were plucked from her hands pretty darn fast.

"The living room is through there," she said, pointing to the doorway on the far end of the kitchen. The sounds of canned laughter from the television seeped out from under the door and she knew Juny and Sue were in there watching TV. Sam would introduce Jane later; no need for everyone to get overwhelmed. "Our classrooms are on the other side of the living room. Tomorrow is Saturday so there are no classes. Though you are welcome to use the computers if you need to."

The computers had all been paid for by Sam's private benefactor two years ago. The modern age took a while to reach Serenity House but now that it was here Sam tried very hard to take care of it.

"And through here—" she turned and opened the swinging door with her butt "—are the bedrooms."

The young girl's eyes were wide, as if she'd not ever thought about the reality of shelters. The shabby cleanliness of it all. The communal reality of women coming together over hardship to make a new start.

Welcome to your new world, Sam thought.

"What kind of classes?" Jane asked, her hand tucked carefully over the small bump of her stomach.

"Computers, reading, clerical. As well as nutrition, child care—"

"Child care?"

Sam nodded, wishing just once a woman would come to this shelter armed with information. Knowledge. But they didn't and when she'd taken over the shelter ten years ago, teaching had become goal one. Not just for the women who lived in the three bedrooms, but for women in the community. They had started coming to the center for classes in droves, once the word got out.

"We've got lots of books, too," Sam said. "Have you been to a doctor?"

Sam saw the lie in the girl's eyes before it came out her mouth, but then something changed. Fear or pride or whatever it was that had put this girl on the road to Serenity House took a backseat and sense took over. "No," she said. "But I feel the baby move all the time."

"That's good," Sam said, turning around to lead Jane

down the small hallway to room three. "But we'll get you set up with a doctor tomorrow."

Jane didn't say thank-you, but Sam could feel the waves of relief that rolled over the girl.

"And here we are." Sam opened the door, revealing a small room with a single bed, table, chair and desk. All used. All well-worn. Like everything else at Serenity House. "It's not much, but it's private and clean. You've been told the rules about drugs and let me reiterate that we're very serious when it comes to prohibiting them."

"I don't do drugs," Jane said.

And where have I heard that before, Sam thought.

"Ohmigod," Jane breathed, the little color she had in her face leaching out. "Don't move."

A low growl rippled down the hall from behind Sam and she smiled, trying to reassure the terrified girl before turning. "Don't worry," she said. "That's Daisy."

"D-D-Daisy?" Jane asked, sounding dubious.

A hundred-pound Rottweiler named Daisy was admittedly ludicrous but Sam thought calling the dog Killer was a bit redundant.

"Come here, Dais," Sam said, holding out her hand to the big black beast that she loved to a stupid degree, for reasons she didn't bother to scrutinize. "Come meet your new duck."

"Duck?" Jane asked, still rattled by the dog. Jane Doe was not a dog person.

"To Daisy you are a duck," Sam said, looking over her shoulder at the girl. "And Daisy takes good care of her ducks."

Understanding dawned in Jane's eyes and she relaxed slightly. Daisy padded up to Sam and held out her nose for a good rub. Sam made the introductions and made sure Daisy got a good noseful of Jane's scent.

The last woman who hadn't met Daisy at the outset found herself pinned to the wall in the middle of the night when she'd come out to use the bathroom. Daisy had stood guard until Sam showed up and called the dog off.

Since then, meeting Daisy became part of the induction process.

"She's a good guard dog," Sam explained. "No one who she doesn't know gets in here. Between Daisy and the patrol car that will be outside you are safe tonight."

"Safe," the girl repeated. "That's good."

Sam knew the concept was foreign to a lot of the women who appeared here, but she couldn't quite get a bead on Jane. Relieved but not grateful. Tough and stubborn. Smart but not smart enough to avoid the situation she was in. She had a sister in school and she knew whoever was looking for her would contact the police. And that thing about her dad really stuck in Sam's craw.

She definitely needed to call in J.D.

Thank God.

Jane took the key from Sam's hand and stepped into her room, a thin young wisp of a girl who was practically swallowed by the shadows.

"Where is your room?" Jane asked. "I mean...will you be here?"

Sam pointed above their heads. "Upstairs," she said. "I'm here all the time."

Nodding, as if that suited her, Jane shut the door and Sam waited until she heard the lock hammer home.

Sam headed to her office to call Chief Bigham. Northwoods was a small town and, outside of a few high-school boys getting drunk and climbing the water tower every summer, Serenity House was the only thing that kept the meager police force busy.

Well, that and the drugs that filtered down from the city on the very highway and train tracks that brought the women searching for Serenity.

But the chief was looking at retirement next year and he didn't do too much about the drugs. And the few times Sam had called looking for some information or help, he'd been less than helpful.

Didn't like to get involved in domestic situations, he said.

"Well, good evening, Samantha," Chief said, after picking up the phone. "What can I do for you tonight?"

"I've got a Jane Doe, Chief."

"You want me to check the computer?"

"No." She knew that him checking the computer was about as helpful as him looking up in the stars for information. "We're calling in our guy on this. I don't want to take up your resources with what might be a wild-goose chase."

Sam figured that if she called J.D. tonight, unless he was already involved in a case, it wouldn't take him too long to get here.

A day. Two.

Jane needed a few days of rest. A chance to see a doctor, get her bearings before Sam dug for more information. She said she hadn't broken any laws and Sam believed her but there was still more to her story. Usually after a night of sleep followed by a good breakfast, the silent girls tended to open up like coin purses.

"I could use some men out front, just in case," she said. It had taken Chief Bigham a while to come around to even the idea of having a car out front when a new woman came to the shelter. But having a homicidal husband track down his family to the shelter—with fatal results—had convinced the chief of the necessity for added protection.

"No problem, Sam. I'll send Paul."

Sam smiled. Paul and Daisy went way back, so the dog should mind her manners. "Thanks, Chief," she said and hung up.

She set the cell phone down on the desk, right in the pool of light cast by the lamp.

Now, she thought, staring at the phone. What to say to J.D.?

I need your help. Oh, and Bob and I broke up. I miss you so much my whole body hurts.

Shaking her head at her own folly, she dialed the number she knew by heart even though she only called him a few times a year.

"J.D.," his strong voice said. "Leave a message."

Sam took a deep breath while the phone beeped. "Hi, J.D., it's me. Sam. We've got a little situation down here and I could use your expertise. Feel free to call me back on my cell. Anytime." *Don't do it. Control yourself, woman.* "Oh, and Bob and I broke up. That's—" *Idiot!* "Yeah, that's all. Talk to you soon."

She disconnected the phone and tossed it on the desk, disgusted with herself and, stupidly, alive with a little thrill.

J.D. was coming to town.

IT TOOK an hour for Sam to complete her nightly walk-through. She was worried about the pipes in the kitchen—the slow leak was becoming more than Deb could fix. And Sam's maintenance budget was down to zero thanks to the last storm that sent a tree through the roof of one of the classrooms.

So she changed the pan under the leak and hoped it would hold until she could discuss budgets with her bookkeeper and determine if she was going to have to call her benefactor.

Glancing out the window over the sink, she saw the patrol car pull up in front of the old oak tree. Paul flashed his lights once, without the siren, then killed the engine.

No moon tonight. No stars.

The dim lights from town shone beyond the trees to the west. Other than that, it was nothing but southern black sky, as far as the eye could see.

Sam wasn't scared of much, and the dark wasn't on the list. But those things that lived in the dark, that threatened her shelter and the women therein, were terrifying.

Made a woman glad to have a hundred-pound killer dog on the premises.

As if reading her mind, Daisy stepped to her side as Sam entered the living room, only to find Juny and her fourteen-year-old daughter, Sue, asleep on the couch in front of the flickering TV.

Curled up like kittens.

She was reluctant to wake the two—both of them slept better with lights on and white noise. But rules were rules. These two women had been their only residents for four months. Sam knew she should have been urging them to move on sooner, but frankly, with so few women staying here these days, Sam felt lonely in the big house. As it was, Juny had gotten a job and the two of them would be leaving bright and early in the morning. Moving out.

Sam smiled, looking at them. Another success story for Serenity.

She sent them, rubbing their eyes, to their bedrooms, and turned off the TV. The darkness followed her through the house, a black cat constantly in her path.

Daisy stayed on the main floor and Sam unlocked her door and climbed the stairs to her rooms on the second floor.

If her office was her headache, her bedroom, kitchen, living room and giant bathroom were her sanctuary. Her grandmother's furniture filled the four rooms she called home, and since her grandmother had had cash and taste, the rooms looked excellent.

She sighed, letting Jane Doe and the pipes slide right off her back along with the white scooped-neck shirt she wore. It puddled on the floor in front of her white-and-red twill couch and she kicked off her red flats by the oak coffee table.

In the doorway of her kitchen she pulled out the pins that held her red hair in a knot and dropped them in her grandmother's cabbage-leaf teacup that was filled with pins and pennies.

Like Daisy after a nap, she gave herself a good hard shake.

Thinking of a hot bath, a cold beer and the possibility of J.D.'s voice in her ear by the end of the night, she unzipped her black skirt and peeled off her tights—noting, with a curse, that the chair with the duct tape had taken a bite out of another pair of black tights.

Wearing just her white bra and pink polka-dotted underwear, she pushed open the door to her deliciously pink, unrepentantly feminine bathroom. Steam spilled out over her feet. Misting over her legs.

"What—"

Her tub was full. Bubbles, a foamy frothy delight of

them, spilled over the lip of her claw-foot tub. The scent of roses was in the hot, humid air.

And sitting, a bit of the dark night condensed, a thrilling spot of masculinity on the closed lid of her toilet, smiling like a man with a secret, was J.D.

2

"You called?" J.D. asked, tilting his head the way Daisy did, the corner of his hard lips lifting.

Her body absorbed him, just soaked him in as though every cell was dying for him. As the steam from the tub pooled around her feet, her body grew damp from the anticipation of what that man, that beautiful man in the worn blue jeans with the devil in his gray eyes, was going to do to her.

It had been so long, she thought, her body weeping.

She opened her mouth, but words had evaporated in the heat radiating from him. It was such a surprise to have him here. She hadn't had time to prepare herself, to wall off her yearning for him so it would be controlled when she saw him. So now it ran loose in her, a wild animal dragging her to places she swore she'd never go again.

So she nodded. But she couldn't move. Couldn't talk.

She tried to restrain the beast, marshal her reaction to him into something appropriate. Something that wouldn't change things between them.

His lips flattened and his face went carefully bland.

Carefully still. "I got the impression from your message that you...ah...were..." He took a deep breath as if trying, as she so often did, to find words to apply to what they had. "Wanting me," he finally said.

Perfect words. Exactly what she felt for him.

His forehead creased and he ran a hand down his thigh. "But maybe I got that wrong."

His body, so lean and strong, coiled as if to move and she didn't want that. Didn't want him going anywhere. So she launched herself across the tiled bathroom and threw herself into his arms, across his lap.

His breath was a gust against her neck, from the force of her body hitting his chest or from relief, she didn't know and she didn't care.

He was staying.

That was all that mattered.

The denim of his jeans electrified the sensitive skin of her inner thighs and when her breasts landed against the taut plane of his chest her whole body lit up like a searchlight.

His hands covered her back, his rough palms holding her tight against him, as though he, too, wanted to absorb her. As though he was all too aware of the time that had passed, the distance that yawned between them, and he wanted to shrink it.

Her blood grew hot, boiling under her skin until her whole body was aflame with the feel of him in her arms. It was better than her millions of fantasies, her lurid daydreams, her raunchy night dreams.

Blood beat like a drum between her legs and she arched against him.

They both groaned at the contact and his hands didn't hold her anymore. They swept over her from the top of her silly, sheer underwear to the sensitive skin at the nape of her neck. He branded it, owned it.

His kiss was wet against her neck, a promise of further delights.

Oh, Lord, he was a living furnace. A muscled heat lamp, so big and strong. She felt small in his arms—a rarity since she was so tall she usually felt like a scarecrow next to men. But not J.D. She could curl up in J.D.'s lap forever, tuck herself in his pocket.

"So I guess I didn't get the message wrong?" J.D. asked, his voice warm and rough in her ear, his breath an equatorial breeze.

"No." She sighed and leaned back, looking into his distinctive eyes. A bright blue band circled the black pupils, fading out to a silver-gray that, right now, glowed from an internal fire. She stroked the black hair off his forehead, longer than the last time she'd seen him. Running her fingers through the new silver that grew at his temples, she wondered what had brought it on.

Where he had been? What he had seen? What his life was like in the months and years they spent apart?

She shook her head, clearing the thoughts that only led down a morose path.

This relationship was of their own design. They didn't ask each other about their lives away from these stolen moments. They didn't ask. They didn't tell. The relationship worked as it was, a bubble that, pressed too hard, would pop.

Feathering her hands along the wide fan of his back, admiring every muscle and bone until she got to the hem of his shirt, she pulled his worn black T-shirt up over his shoulders. He released her briefly so she could yank the T-shirt over his head and throw it on the floor behind her. She trailed her fingers over his chest, the smooth hairless muscles and bones.

"What's this?" she asked, finding a new scar, a thin jagged line that bisected his left nipple.

"Nothing," he said, his voice gravelly.

She hummed a negative response, knowing they'd talk about it later, and pressed a kiss to the raised cut, found his nipple and licked it.

His clever fingers unhooked her bra, tossing it away, releasing her breasts into his palms, his rough thumbs a welcome violence against the sensitive skin of her nipples. He cupped her, lifted her and, as she'd known he would, he sucked her. Used his tongue. His teeth. Nothing soft. Nothing gentle. No sweet hellos. No careful reintroduction.

It was always this way between them. Fast and faster. Hot and hotter.

She gasped, rolling against his crotch, throwing gasoline on the flames.

His laugh was dark, familiar, and it trickled right though her skin to the core of her, amping up the furnace that raged between them.

One of his big, rough hands left her breast. The backs of his fingers stroked her stomach.

He delicately traced the scar on her belly and she squeezed her eyes shut at the touch. *Don't ask. Don't ask.*

And he didn't. He never did. His hand slid down, farther, until he cupped the damp heat of her, his fingers tracing her through her underwear.

Her legs twitched, her head rolled back on a neck too weak to support her.

"I'm glad you called me," he whispered in her ear, taking the lobe between his teeth. His fingers continued their wicked dance. "I'm always glad when you call me."

She gasped, words beyond her. No one ever had this power over her. One touch. One word growled in her ear and she was ready for him.

Her hips pulsed against his. Aware of his erection and the fact that he loved to tease her and would do it all night if she let him, she palmed the front of his pants, pressing the heel of her hand to the turgid length of him.

He groaned and she smiled, loving everything about this. Loving how wrong it was. How delicious it was to have this man groaning and straining beneath her.

He laughed, dipping one finger into her then pulling away when she arched toward him to take more.

She thrust her fingers through his hair, the animals of lust and yearning stampeding through her body. She couldn't take his teasing tonight. She didn't want games. She simply wanted him.

"Please," she said into eyes that flashed silver with erotic understanding.

He blinked at her, leaned up to kiss her with his eyes wide open.

How can he do that? she wondered. Unable to bear the intimacy she shut her own eyes with a sigh.

He pressed a condom into her hand and she ripped it open while he opened his jeans. It was a slick dance between them, flawless as if they'd done it all yesterday.

Her underwear was yanked aside, the filmy fabric ripping under his rough hands. The sound of the rending fabric utterly thrilled her.

And then, there he was, hard and heavy, a spear right through her. Erasing the past seven months, three weeks and two days since she'd last taken him in her body.

∼

"So?" He asked, two condoms, a tub of cold water, two beers and an hour and a half later. Sam leaned back in his arms, floating slightly in the bathwater and on a cloud of J.D. A lovely little puff of boneless, I-just-got-laid contentment. "What happened with Bob?"

"Bob." She took a sip of her beer and stalled until he rested the bottom of his cold bottle on her bare shoulder. She yipped and sat up slightly, her feet hitting the far end of her big tub.

But he pulled her back, laughing, and settled her against his chest.

"It didn't work out," she finally said and felt his chest vibrate from his laugh. He was always so loose after making love, as though he'd finally thrown off the chains of his job.

It made her want to cuddle him.

They didn't often talk about his work, but she knew he took it seriously. And she knew he was good at it. A knight in denim for a lot of people who needed his services. Lord knew he'd been that and more since she took over Serenity House ten years ago. She'd found his name in her mentor's Rolodex with the note "good guy to call if there's trouble."

And trouble had landed fast by way of a woman showing up, beaten, no ID, a wad of cash and claiming to have been raped by a U.S. senator.

The cops had been useless, the woman had been terrified, and unsure of what else to do—Sam had called J.D.

And, in the end, the senator had done some time thanks to the evidence J.D. was able to find.

It was the first of many times he'd come to her rescue over the years.

"Hey, Sam. I respect your privacy if you don't want to talk about it."

She turned, slipping slightly on the bottom of the tub, so

she could see his face. Hard and dangerous with a splotch of bubbles dripping off his chin.

Oh, if the bad guys could see him now.

"You have such pretty eyes," she said, staring into that blue-gray spectrum.

"Don't change the subject," he said. "It seemed serious." He lifted his eyebrows and took another swig from his bottle.

She laughed. "Serious because I didn't sleep with you when you came through town three months ago?"

"Yeah," he said, point-blank. "It's been ten years, Sam. And you've never said no—"

"You haven't either." She didn't like that she was so easy for him, but loved that he was so easy for her.

"No." He shook his head, so solemn. "I haven't. But you did for that guy."

She'd actually said no for a lot of reasons, the least of which was Bob. After ten years of this confusing, no-strings, no future relationship, she'd decided enough was enough.

And now look at you, she thought. *Back in the bathtub with him.* But she couldn't work up much self-flagellation. She'd been screwed silly.

"He wanted to get married," she said, surprising herself by confessing the truth.

J.D. cocked his head, his face giving away nothing. If he was surprised he didn't show it. He didn't show much. "You don't?" he asked.

She shook her head and turned around, gliding right back into that spot between his legs, his pubic hair feathering against her lower back. His chest the best pillow for her head ever made.

"Well, then," he said, his voice low and right in her ear

and suddenly it wasn't just pubic hair at her back. "Too bad for Bob."

His hand slid under the water, his arm vanishing into the realm of bubbles and secrets. He cupped her breast and she sighed. His fingers grazed her scar and she tensed.

"You okay?" he asked and she wanted to kick herself. She forgot about the scar for the ninety-eight percent of her life when he wasn't around. It was like her nose or something, just one of the parts that made up the whole.

But when J.D. was around that scar bisecting her belly seemed to be lined in neon.

A regret about her decision nine years ago danced around her periphery. Would things be different if she'd told him? Would there be more between them? Did she want more between them?

But, she reminded herself, yanking herself away from those thoughts. She didn't want more. This was perfect. Those other things—kids, marriage, family—were cards she didn't even want in her deck.

She'd made the right decision. In fact, she made the right decision every time she let J.D. walk back out of her life.

"I'm fine," she said.

His fingers found her under the water, slick and swollen from just being near him. She jumped slightly at the electrical pulse between his fingers and her clitoris, so J.D. hooked his legs around her, spreading her open, keeping her still while his fingers worked their magic.

SAM MADE THEM HAM SANDWICHES. She always made them ham sandwiches. He always sat on her counter, wearing his boxers. And she wore her Chinese silk robe, feeling very Rizzo and sexy and lady of the world as she sliced ham and broke off pieces of iceberg lettuce.

"Do you eat when you're not here?" she asked, handing him his third sandwich. She eyed his wiry strength, his lean-cut muscles that bordered on skinny.

"Not much," he said, grinning at her.

"How'd you get in without me hearing you?" she asked.

"I have a key, remember? You gave it to me."

"I meant," she said, shooting him an arch look, "how did you get past Daisy?"

"Every private investigator knows how to deal with dogs."

"Oh, no, not treats." She groaned. "I told you it makes her sick—"

"She knows me, Sam," he said. "She used to be mine, remember?"

Of course. J.D. brought Daisy to Sam when Eva and her daughter had been killed by her ex-husband eight months ago. Eight months ago when she'd lost her mind in grief and worry and called him, not for business, but because she'd needed him.

And he came. He brought Daisy. Stayed for three days. On the fourth morning she woke up alone. Well, not entirely alone. Daisy snored on the floor by her bed.

Serenity's first guard dog.

A few weeks later Sam finally agreed to date Bob.

The reasons for that decision she didn't really like to think about.

"So what's the story with your Jane Doe?" J.D. asked, his eyes shifting slightly into focus. Loverman was fading as J. D. Kronos, P.I., took over.

Which was good, because the memories she worked so

hard to pretend didn't exist were playing like a movie in her head. Half-naked Loverman, with the wicked fingers and beautiful eyes, made her wish things were different.

"Came in tonight. No ID. She's lying about her age. She's six months pregnant and scared out of her mind." Sam sat down at her red-and-silver dinette and bit into her own sandwich. She reconsidered the mayo and added some.

"Drugs?"

"Not that Deb or I could tell."

"Abuse?"

She shook her head. "Again, not that we could tell. I imagine I'll get more from her tomorrow morning. She's smart, though. And she doesn't look like a street kid. She's got a diamond around her neck that would keep her in meth for a month. Or at a suite at the Hilton, if all she really wanted to do was piss off her folks. But she hasn't sold it. She's wearing expensive jeans. She's clean, her skin is good. She's got great teeth."

His eyebrows lifted as if he understood how alarming that was. Usually, the first appointment Sam scheduled for the women that came to the shelter was a dentist. Years of never visiting a dentist, a terrible diet, poor hygiene and possible drugs took a real toll on the teeth.

Not Jane Doe's. Sam would bet the girl was fresh out of braces.

"Any sense of where she's from?"

"Not here," she said. "There's an accent could be New York or Jersey. Maybe Philly. Or—" she sighed "—it could be a put-on. Dad's involved and not in a good way."

Something in him changed. His body flexed, his muscles alert. "How old?"

"Seventeen tops."

"Blond?" he asked, held his hand up to his shoulder. "Hair this long?"

She shook her head, charged by whatever electrical current was running though him. "Chin-length and she's dyed it black. Why?"

"I don't know," he answered, polishing off the sandwich in one big bite. "Might be nothing." He jumped off the counter. "But I can check my laptop and—" He groaned. "How is your wireless these days?"

Sam smiled. "Same as it always is." Which meant terrible up here. It was like the second floor was a bunker or something.

"You need a new modem."

"I need a lot of things. But I'll go reset the modem."

He grabbed a shirt and she watched him shamelessly, all those muscles flexing, while he pulled it on then ran a hand through his black hair.

Bracing one hand on the table in front of her and the other on the back of her chair, he kissed her nose, licked the corner of her mouth where mayonnaise must have been caught. "You look tired," he said. "Why don't you stay here and get some sleep. I'll be quiet. The women won't even know I'm here."

She smiled up at him, touched by his concern—actually utterly knocked out by it, since concern wasn't something people felt about her.

He was such a good man, seeing what other people didn't. Offering what she didn't even realize she needed.

But this was her job. Her home. Those women her responsibility. "I'll come with you."

He nodded as if he approved of her decision. "Lead on," he said with a grin that winged through her.

It was well past midnight and the chances of any of the

women being up were slim to none, but she couldn't risk someone losing their minds when they saw J.D., dark and masculine, skulking through the shadows.

He grabbed his laptop and followed Sam barefoot down the stairs to the kitchen.

With him at her back, her body sore from the delicious intrusion of lovemaking, and her mind wiped clean of worry, she felt everything a bit sharper. As if a layer of skin had been rubbed away by his hands.

The night had finally cooled and a draft rolled up from the open windows in the kitchen. The smooth oak stairs felt like silk under her bare feet and the distinctive blended smell that was her home—of roses from upstairs and disinfectant from downstairs—filled the air.

The creak of the door as she pushed into the shadowy kitchen was slightly eerie, foreboding.

The fridge door was open, a bright slice of yellow light taken out of the darkness. And at the sound of Sam and J.D. stepping into the kitchen, Jane Doe, her mouth full of cake from Sue's birthday yesterday, whirled.

Sam held up her hand, reading bloodcurdling panic on the girl's face. "It's okay," Sam said, rushing around the table. "He's a friend."

But it was too late. J.D. was at her back and with one look at him Jane dropped the cake to the floor.

"I know you!" Jane breathed, pointing a hand at J.D. Her entire body vibrated, her eyes rolling white in fear. "He sent you, didn't he?" Jane cried.

3

In J.D.'s line of work he often got mistaken as the bad guy. Fair enough. He often was. But not this time. He hadn't been sent for Jane Doe. And while Sam tried to chill the girl out in her room, J.D. used his resources to suss out the real bad guy.

And he really, really hoped it wasn't Francis "Frank" Conti.

But his gut was telling him there was a pretty good chance Jane was the daughter of the most bloodthirsty capo in the Gamboni crime family.

Sam's luck was like that.

J.D. scanned the Polaroid of Jane that Deb had taken when signing the girl in to Serenity House, and opened his e-mail.

Greg Spili worked the FBI Organized Crime Unit out of Newark, and he and J.D. were friendly enough when Greg wasn't being a pain in the ass about their childhood in Newark. He would be able to ID the photo and confirm or deny the rumors that had been circulating about Christina Conti's disappearance.

Even though he wished it wasn't true, J.D. looked at that photo and knew it was Christina.

She had her father's nose, unfortunately.

There was no way she knew him, despite what she said in the kitchen. She hadn't even been born when J.D. did that job for her father twenty years ago.

Fear that her father was sending someone after her and the resemblance he probably had to any one of the thugs her father had for hire, had been what she was responding to.

He just hoped Sam believed that.

Greg, he wrote, the clack of the keyboard loud in the quiet room. Friend of mine picked up this Jane Doe and I'm thinking she's your missing girl. She is still missing, right? Contact me ASAP. I've got a bad feeling about this. J.D.

He hit Send and wondered who else would be looking for her. If this really was Christina, J.D. guessed there would be a reward for finding her.

If he reached out would Conti would greet him with open arms or a bullet in the back of the head? It had been years since J.D. worked for Conti, but the guy had a memory like an elephant. A big, dumb, violent elephant.

He hoped whoever was looking for Christina wouldn't find her anytime soon.

He checked his watch and scrubbed a hand over his head.

It was 1:00 a.m. Lord, he was tired. He'd been an hour outside Baltimore when he got Sam's message. He'd spent the past week confirming what a lawyer had already known to be true—the lawyer's wife was screwing his best friend in shabby hotel rooms all around D.C.

J.D. had been tired then. But, as usual, the sound of Sam's voice on his answering machine made him do things that didn't make sense. Worse this time since she'd tacked on that bit about breaking up with Bob.

And so, instead of getting a hotel room for a few hours' sleep then calling her, he'd pressed his foot to the floor and sped the whole way here. And with each mile he'd shed his skin, his life, his job and all the damn ghosts, until he'd arrived at her door with nothing but what he felt for Sam.

He was just J. D. Kronos and Sam didn't ask for anything more.

He would drive for days if the destination was Sam's bedroom.

The chair squealed under his shifting weight and he swore when his leg hair got caught in the duct tape on the side.

The woman needed to throw the thing out. But he smiled, knowing why she didn't. It still worked, was still useful. Sam wrung every ounce of use out of things before getting rid of them. When the chair stopped operating as a chair she'd probably turn it into a lawn ornament or something.

The woman was practical right down to, but excluding, her frilly, sexy, girly underwear.

Suddenly, J.D. wasn't so tired anymore.

He closed his computer, letting it hibernate with Sam's modem still plugged in. He'd check mail first thing in the morning and see if they couldn't get this Jane Doe situation put to bed.

But right now he'd like to put Sam to bed.

Out of habit he walked along the darkest parts of the shadows, his elbows grazing the wall, his feet inches from the baseboards.

The kitchen was empty, but the light in the hallway toward the bedrooms was still on. He imagined Sam was trying to stop Jane from running away, which seemed like such a waste of time. Such a lot of work to fight something that was probably going to happen anyway.

Young, pregnant Jane Does rarely had a happy ending.

But there would be no telling Sam that.

He cleaned up the cake on the floor and headed upstairs to wait for Sam.

THE CREAK of the floor woke J.D. and he sat up as if launched by a slingshot from the couch he'd fallen asleep on. The room was dark but roses perfumed the air and he knew Sam was back.

Her scent filled his head and weariness vanished. He stepped from the couch, tracking her silently to the kitchen where she stood looking out the window over the sink.

Silver moonlight gilded her.

Her hair, all those long red waves were piled up on her head in some kind of messy, intricate knot. The cream silk of her robe slid up her muscled arms as she drank from a glass of water. The ivory of her skin matched the robe that covered her body, so tall, so perfect and strong.

I wish...

The chains of his reality, his past, his future, the bleak and dismal present, jerked him away from finishing that sentence. He had no business wishing anything about Sam. Other than that Bob had worked out for her. And J.D. really did wish Bob had.

She needed someone who could give her what she deserved. Love, a family, hearth and home and all that shit.

A woman like Sam shouldn't go through life alone, carrying what she shouldered on a daily basis. She could do it, had done it for ten years and, knowing her, she'd go on doing it for another twenty more.

But she deserved more.

Instead, she had him, twice, maybe three times a year. Sex, sandwiches and what little help he could provide. He wished he could give her more. Was the kind of man who could be what she needed.

But he wasn't.

Instead, he smiled, thinking of her skin, her breasts, the wonderland of her sex. He was more than happy to give her what she wanted.

He made sure to make some noise when he stepped onto the kitchen's linoleum and she turned, startled.

She'd been lost in thought, no doubt about Jane Doe and her reaction to him, and that bothered him. Rattled the chains that bound him.

"J.D.?" she whispered, watching him with her brown eyes that appeared almost black in the moonlight. A hundred questions were in her eyes. A thousand unasked inquiries.

Guilt buzzed through him. She didn't know him. She thought she did, he could see it in her sometimes after they made love. She'd look at him and think he was some kind of Prince Charming. A white knight.

A good guy.

But he wasn't. And the proof was that he never set her straight. Because if he did, she wouldn't allow him to touch her.

Selfish bastard, a fraud, through and through.

The man she thought he was, the man she saw in his eyes, didn't exist. J. D. Kronos didn't exist.

As he stared at her, her lips parted. Her breath came faster. He watched as her nipples under the silk went hard.

"Everything okay with Jane Doe?" he asked, getting rid of business before he dealt with that body of hers.

The air in the kitchen was humid from the fire that burned between them.

"She's calmed down, but it took a while. She was ready to run. She had so many questions about you." Sam sighed, and ran a hand over her hair, her face.

And I didn't have the answers. He knew that was what she was thinking and he felt a certain inevitability wash over him. She was going to ask the questions now. The questions they never asked. The questions that would bring this whole thing down.

Ten years. It had been good while it lasted. He would miss Sam. He would miss being her J.D.

A sizzling startling pain ricocheted through his body.

He never thought it would last forever but he had hoped... God, it didn't matter anymore.

"J.D.," she whispered, her gaze rock solid, unwavering. "She thought she knew you. She thought—"

He shook his head because he wanted her, one more time. Needed her. One more night. So, he stepped toward her, pressing her against the fridge, a mere inch of superheated air between them.

"Do you really want to talk about that?" he asked. "Right now?"

"J.D.—"

He kissed her, licked her mouth. Brushed her nipples with his thumbs until he felt the resistance in her melt. Pressing his hips to hers, she finally sighed and gave in, wrapping her arms around his neck.

This is the last time, he thought. *It's got to be.*

He'd said that before over the years, but this was different.

Desperate suddenly for her body, her kiss, her naked skin, he picked her up and took her to her bedroom, hoping dawn, and her inevitable questions, could be delayed.

SAM STARED out her window and waited for the coffee to brew. Dawn was a pink light over the horizon and the air was already heavy with the beginnings of humidity. Somehow Sam had a feeling that this was going to be a very bad day.

She had stayed up most of the night watching J.D. sleep and counting on both hands the concrete things she knew about him.

He was a good lover. He was a P.I. His name was Jonathon David. He was thirty-seven. And...she thought maybe he had some sisters.

That was it. And last night when Jane had taken one look at him and gone white, Sam realized that it would behoove her and maybe Jane Doe to find out a little bit more.

Around 3:00 a.m. everything she didn't know about him became suspicious. How did he get here so fast last night? Within two hours? It was as if he were on his way. And why would Jane think he'd been sent for her? Had she seen him somewhere? Did she know him?

All things Sam should have asked. Probably before she had sex with him, but better late than never. Not asking him questions was a habit she didn't know how to break.

But it was time.

The coffeemaker gurgled its last and Sam poured two mugs full. She added a little sugar to his because that's the way he liked it.

There, she thought triumphantly. *That's five concrete things I know. J.D. likes sugar in his coffee.*

But it didn't make her feel better.

Who has an affair with a man for ten years without knowing his birthday? Or his favorite color? Or if he's been hired by Jane Doe's father to find her?

At the sound of her pushing open the bedroom door, J.D. snapped upright from the sound sleep she'd left him in.

"Hi," she said, handing him his mug, trying to avert her eyes from his chest. His groin where her ladybug sheets didn't quite hide his morning erection.

"Hi yourself." His voice was a gravel road. His smile a hundred-percent invitation.

Why am I so nervous about this? she wondered, as the butterflies in her stomach got butterflies in their stomachs. *It's not like I'm accusing him of anything, or asking him to tell me about his past girlfriends. Or even current ones, should he have them.*

And wasn't that a pleasant thought.

She just needed to know if he knew Jane Doe. If he was, in fact, after Jane Doe.

"What time is it?" he asked, looking out at the brightening sky.

Time to answer some questions, she thought. "A little past seven," she said and he groaned.

She sucked in the warm air of her bedroom, felt the heat of sunlight from the big windows at her back. It was peaceful here, a sanctuary, and she had thought it was that way for him, too.

But what did she know? Really?

"We need to talk," she said and it was as if she'd pulled a gun on him.

His body tightened, his face shut down. All that sleepy,

sexy happiness that had been in his eyes vanished as if it had never been there.

"We don't talk," he said, taking a sip of coffee. Not totally true. When he was here they talked a lot. About College football. And books. Music. They talked politics.

But they didn't talk about *them*.

"I know we *haven't*," she said. "But I think...we should. I have some questions. About last night. About Jane Doe."

They both watched his thumb stroke the handle of his mug. "You can't go back," he said, his voice low and somehow ominous. "Once you do this."

Dread fell hard upon her shoulders. He was hiding something. "I know," she said, trying to pretend she didn't understand exactly what he meant. "But we're friends, right?"

He didn't say anything. He didn't even nod and a thin ribbon of disbelief trickled through her bloodstream. This man, the one in her bed who had gone down on her last night until she saw stars, was a stranger.

Sam stood, paced to the window to get some distance. A little clarity. "I think considering the way Jane reacted to you last night, I would be pretty negligent if I didn't ask you some questions."

He blinked once. Processing her accusation. "You mean when she asked if I'd been sent for her?"

"Yes."

"She reacted to me because I am a man and she's scared. And she knows whoever she's running from probably will send someone after her."

God, it sounded so reasonable when he put it that way. It was like running into a brick wall. But she knew when she was right, and this was right.

"I understand that," she said. "But it was as if she recognized you. She said she knew you."

"I was in the shadows," he said. "There was no way she could have seen my face."

"You could have been hired by someone to find her."

"I wasn't."

That was it. He took another sip of coffee and her mouth fell open. He was so calm, so cool, turning away her questions like a loans officer or someone equally impersonal.

"But you do know who she is?" She stepped closer, ready to drag some honesty out of him, if just to satisfy her pride.

"I have some ideas but a colleague will get back to me today."

"What kind of colleague? A cop?"

"Not really."

She jerked away, stupidly injured to realize he didn't respect her enough to be honest.

"Hey," he said, reaching for her arm, but she didn't let him touch her. "I'm not lying."

"But you're not telling me the truth either," she said, blinking at him, stunned that a man could share so much and still be an utter mystery. She had a responsibility to the women of Serenity House and she'd thought he understood that. Respected that.

She pulled the collar of her robe up slightly higher.

"Don't do that. Don't act injured. You have your share of secrets too. It's how this whole thing between us works."

"I know. But, right now I'm confused and worried and to be honest, feeling a bit stupid for spreading my legs for a man who clearly doesn't respect me enough to answer the most basic questions."

His face turned to stone and he set the mug down on the bedside table with a thunk before plucking his underwear from the floor. "Why don't you ask me the question you really want to ask?" he said, drilling her to the wall with his gaze.

She swallowed. "Who are you?"

"You know who I am."

She shook her head, suddenly all too aware that she didn't. At all.

"I'm a private investigator," he said. "I have contacts who are cops and contacts who are doing life at Rikers. I get paid to sneak around at night and confirm everyone's worst suspicions about their loved ones. Is that what you want to know?"

"No," she said. "Well, yes. But your work—"

"Do you want me to tell you that I only work for the good guys? That I would never work for Jane Doe's father? That I wouldn't put that girl downstairs in danger because someone paid me money?"

"I guess, yes."

"Then the answer is no. No, I work for bad guys a lot of the time. And maybe Jane recognized me because I might have done some work for whoever is chasing her. And if someone hired me to find Jane Doe, I'd still be here and I'd do my job."

And you. The words, unsaid, hung in the air.

I would betray you, was what he really meant. Without thinking twice.

"You wouldn't," she said, believing it to her core. The man who drew hot baths for her, held her while she slept, loved her sometimes as if she were precious wouldn't hurt her, not deliberately.

"I would."

"No." She shook her head. "You—"

"Stop, Sam. I'm not your white knight."

"I never said you were."

"But you thought it. You wished it."

That was the truth. And she couldn't deny it. She had an image of him that he was taking a sledgehammer to and she didn't understand why.

"Okay, what about you?" he asked.

She stilled, every muscle tense. "What about me?"

"Why are you doing this?"

"Asking you questions? Because—"

"Sleeping with me. Or, wait, how did you put it, 'spreading your legs'?"

Oh. Ouch.

She tossed her hair over her shoulder, lifted her chin, armoring herself with the truth. "Because I can't stop," she said. Even when she knew she should. Even though she kept a terrible secret from him and he no doubt kept millions of them from her.

"Do you want to stop?" he asked. The fire in his eyes was banked, his face so carefully bland. No emotion. No indication of what he wanted. No sign of her lover.

Just a stranger in her bedroom.

She swallowed, everything numb below her hairline. "I don't want to change what we have," she said. "But I suddenly realized last night that what I don't know about you is slightly scary."

"You're scared of me?" he asked, and for the first time since starting this awful conversation, he seemed to register a real human emotion.

"I'm scared of what I don't know about you."

They stared at each other, another one of those showdowns that she usually won. And she wished she could keep her mouth shut until he made some kind of explanation. But she couldn't.

"I've trusted you," she whispered. She thought of when Eva and her daughter had been killed, when Sam had called J.D. and he'd come, bringing sex and understanding and a guard dog. *I've loved you*, she thought, knowing it to be true, and felt as if she were cutting off an arm. "I've trusted you with the women who come here, with their lives, their information. I've trusted you with my home. My body."

"It's just sex, Sam."

It was as if he'd slapped her.

It was as if he'd hauled off and punched her in the gut.

She turned before he could see her cry, staring out the window at the willow in the front yard until it blurred and swam in the tears pooling in her eyes.

The hands that wiped them away shook.

Since she wasn't an idiot, she didn't argue. It was just sex, in black and white. But she'd grown to believe over the years that there was something more. A communion between them. An unspoken...care. A delight and respect in the other's self that went beyond sex.

Well, I guess I was wrong.

She opened her mouth to tell him to leave, but the shrill blast of her phone ringing interrupted.

Relieved, she left him and her bedroom for the phone in the kitchen.

"Hello," she croaked, her voice thick with tears and pain.

"Hey, Sam," Deb said from the phone downstairs. "I hate bugging you when I know you got J.D. going on up—"

"It's all right. What's going on?" Sam asked, pinching her nose as a headache blew up behind her eyes.

"Sue and Juny left a couple of things when they moved out this morning. Said they'd be back to get them."

"Is that all?"

"No, Ms. Happy, it isn't. I've got a woman down here asking for you."

"Is she looking for help?"

Deb laughed. "This lady don't need our help. She could sell her watch and fix our plumbing problems. She said she's got some business with you about something that happened nine years ago. A letter or something?"

None of that made sense, but considering the short-circuiting in her brain, the alphabet was a mystery right now.

"I'll be down in ten minutes."

She hung up and turned, only to find J.D., shirtless, his pants unzipped, arms braced wide on the frame of the kitchen door.

It's just sex, she reminded herself when her heart surged at the sight of him. *That's all you are to him.*

She'd seen enough self-destructive behavior in her life to know when she was beginning to walk down that path. And wanting to get back in bed with him after the conversation they'd just had was as self-destructive as it got.

She stepped toward him, but he didn't budge.

"I have to go to work," she said. "Let me by."

"Look at me, Sam," he said, his voice soft, and she couldn't help but comply.

"I'm sorry," he murmured, his stunning blue-gray eyes contrite. "I am. I'm not good at answering questions. Or talking. Really. You...ah...caught me by surprise."

Sam laughed, but it was an ugly sound, full of hurt and anger. "You and me both. I need to get dressed." After a moment, he stepped aside and she went into her room and shut the door between them.

JENNIFER STERN HAD a spot on her shirt. A big fat coffee stain right over the second button on her cream blouse. And of all the catastrophes that had befallen her in the past six months, the fact that she was about to have this meeting covered in spilled coffee seemed the worst.

And the fact that this meeting was about to happen in a supply closet added insult to injury. Sure, there were two chairs and a desk, but Jennifer knew a supply closet when she was forced to wait in one.

She wanted to cry. And she hadn't cried for months.

"Mom?" Spence rested against her knee, wedged between the desk and a box of what looked like shower curtains. His nine-year-old body smelled of sunshine and doughnuts. He wasn't spotted or stained, though. No, he was in his best clothes, his red curls slightly more managed than usual.

He even wore his good shoes without complaint. He'd drawn the line at the tie she'd brought along and she had to concede that her efforts to make him a walking, talking testimony to her mothering skills had to end somewhere.

But he was healthy, polite, smart as a whip. Confident and silly. Kind. Inquisitive and serious at times to the point of hair-pulling frustration.

But most importantly he was hers.

And she would die before she gave him up.

"Yeah, hon?" She didn't stroke his head as she wanted to because she knew that he'd shrug her off. Too old, too cool for such things.

"What are we gonna do?" he asked.

Jennifer bit her lip to stop from laughing. Now he wonders? When they were sitting in this office, her covered in coffee, him smelling of Dunkin' Donuts?

Admittedly she wasn't much better. In fact, she'd only

started to come up with a game plan this morning, after finding out that Samantha Riggins did still live at the address she'd left on file nine years ago.

What were the chances really?

A thirty-eight-year-old woman staying in the same place for nine years. It was unheard-of. From the age of twenty-eight Jennifer had moved no less than ten times, working her way up the ladder of television news.

And because she never, ever thought this meeting would actually happen, Jennifer had concocted a speech for Spence regarding the way people change and grow up and leave things behind, to help him get over the fact that he wouldn't be able to meet Samantha.

But now they were about to meet her.

I am breaking so many rules, she thought, stunned that she was even capable of that. There were regulations she as the adoptive mother was supposed to follow. And here she was in this closet, ignoring every single one of them.

What's happened to me? she wondered, panicked and scared of who she was becoming.

And if Jennifer had been able to foresee this particular moment—complete with coffee stain and closet—she would have told Spence no when he brought this adventure up.

"Mommy," he'd said solemnly two weeks ago, "I think it's time for me to meet her."

"I mean, do we just tell her?" he asked now.

She shook her head. "I don't think that would be very nice to her, do you? Just springing it on her like that? What do you think we should do?"

"Well." He dug his notebook out of his knapsack. The grief counselor had told Spence to write things down and the boy, in his usual fashion, had taken her advice to heart.

That notebook was the first thing he picked up in the morning and the last thing he put down at night. "I have some questions for her."

Jennifer's mouth unfroze from the perpetual frown she had these days and she felt the brief warmth of a smile. "I'm sure you do, sweetie. But I think maybe what would be best is if I talk to her first for a few minutes. Just to tell her who we are and what we're doing here. Then you can ask her questions."

"What do you think she looks like?"

"I don't know," she answered. She tried to cross her legs but hit the desk with her shin. "We'll soon find out, won't we?" She tried to sound excited because Spence was.

"Hey, Mom."

"Yeah, hon?"

"Do you think she'll like me?" he asked, blinking owlishly at her.

The tears she'd been fighting since spilling her coffee clawed at the back of her eyes and she had to bite her tongue hard enough to draw blood to keep them at bay.

"I do," she finally said. "It's impossible not to." She sighed. "But if you don't like her, we'll leave right away." She ducked her head to better see his face. He'd been so brave for the past year. And so excited the whole drive down, only now to be stricken with fear and doubt.

She pulled him into her arms and he let her. He let her stroke his hair and press a kiss to his sweaty forehead, which only told her how nervous her boy was.

"I love you," she said.

"I know," he whispered.

Finally the door opened. A tall woman in a black top and khaki pants stood in the doorway.

She had red hair.

Spencer gets his hair from her, Jennifer thought, feeling a little more of her heart break.

Jennifer put her hand against her son's trembling back. He was practically vibrating. And she realized this was too much. There were a million things Jennifer should have done before this meeting, protocols she should have followed. But none of that seemed important or real.

She'd driven down here thinking this was simply a road trip that would end with her son's brief disappointment. But now they were looking possible heartbreak in the face.

More heartbreak.

And suddenly it became too late to go home. Too late to change course.

"I'm sorry to keep you waiting," she said. Sam was her name. Samantha Riggins. Sam glanced at Spence and he stiffened as if caught by high beams. Jennifer saw his face go pale. But Sam only smiled, missing every sign of Spence's distress. "Maybe you want to go into the kitchen with Deb?" Sam asked, turning slightly, revealing the black woman sporting the long thin braids with blond tips who had talked to them when they arrived.

Spence grabbed Jennifer's hand and shook his head, clearly not wanting to go anywhere with anyone. Jennifer stroked his back, trying to calm his sudden fear.

"You sure?" Sam asked. "Breakfast is being served."

"We talked about this, babe," Jennifer whispered in his ear, though she wished she could capitalize on these sudden misgivings of his and pick him up and go, take him to a Waffle House and forget this closet ever existed.

But she'd promised him. And worse. She'd promised Doug. "I just need a few minutes with her," Jennifer said.

His gray-blue eyes swam with indecision and fear. *I don't want to leave you, Mommy*, his eyes said and she swallowed the lump of indecision and fear that lodged in her own throat.

"It's okay," she promised. "I swear. If it starts getting good —" she smiled, knowing his theory that all the good stuff was adult stuff "—I'll call you in."

Spence gave Sam one more hard look as if cataloging all the things they had in common. Then he pursed his lips as if gathering all his courage and glanced down at his notebook.

"I'm allergic to strawberries," he said to Sam.

"I...ah...don't think we're serving strawberries," Sam said. "So you're safe."

"Are you allergic to anything?" he asked.

"Shrimp," Sam answered. "They give me hives."

They did the same thing to Spence and he checked something off on his notebook before tucking it back in his backpack, looking satisfied.

My baby, Jennifer's heart cried. *My sweet little guy.*

"Do you have doughnuts?" he asked Deb. Sam laughed but Jennifer couldn't. If she laughed she'd bawl.

"Maybe," Deb answered, holding out her hand. "Let's go find out." Spence didn't take the stranger's hand but he followed her out the door, his ginger curls gilded by the sun in front of him, his khaki pants inches too long.

"Now," Sam sighed, sitting in her chair with the duct tape and, come to find out, a terrible squeal. "What can I help you with?"

"I'm afraid it's complicated," Jennifer said, totally unsure of where to start.

"Isn't it always?" Sam said with a smile. "But Deb told me you'd mentioned a letter?"

Jennifer took a deep breath, cursed her husband and

deathbed promises, then jumped into a situation she'd fought for the past nine years.

"The letter, I, ah...referred to...is the letter you left in your file with the adoption agency."

Sam didn't speak. Her brows furrowed and she shook her head as if she just didn't follow.

Stupid woman, Jennifer thought unkindly. *Did Spence mean nothing to her?*

"The permission to contact letter you wrote when you gave your son up for adoption."

Understanding struck the woman's face and she went pale. White pale. Even her lips lost all their color. Her hand shook as she brought it to her forehead. "Oh, my God," she whispered and turned slightly toward the door Spence just walked out of. "Your son—"

"Well, biologically—" Jennifer nearly choked on the words "—Spence is your son."

4

There was a giant empty vacuum where thought should be. Sam knew she should say something. Anything. But she opened her mouth and there were no words. A rattling dry gasp from the back of her throat, that's all.

My son. Here.

Feeling cornered, she pushed away from her desk, the chair rolling into the boxes of soap behind her, and she felt the other woman's eyes on her, watching her.

What was the right way to respond? Or feel, for that matter. Because all Sam had was shock, blind and all-consuming. Her feet were numb, her hands blocks of ice.

"Perhaps this is a bad time?" the tense woman said and Sam finally focused, the roar in her ears abating for the moment.

"What's your name?" Sam asked, courtesy a luxury that had been blown off the map.

"Jennifer," the woman said. Her blond hair was practically a mirror, it was so straight and pale and perfect. "Jennifer Stern. I am Spence's mother."

"Right." It was all she could say. Words had utterly escaped her. Through the great nothing she felt, panic crept in, crawling over her and through her like stinging fog.

She couldn't breathe.

My son. Here.

What should I do? Say? Oh, Christ, what do I say to him?

The ceiling above her head creaked while J.D. moved around upstairs and horror broke over her like a thunderstorm.

Oh, my God.

Her heart stopped dead cold in her chest.

The reality of the situation hammered her right in the stomach.

J.D.

What were the chances that her son and J.D. would be here at the same time? What were the seriously cosmically screwed-up odds on that event?

After all these years, and worse, after that conversation this morning, he was going to learn her secret.

Spence was his son, too.

"Perhaps we should come back," Jennifer said, so disapproving, so cool she might have been made of ice.

Yes. Leave. I can't do this today. The words leaped to Sam's lips, but she swallowed the words and took deep breaths.

Did she want to push away this chance? Because of timing?

That had been her rationale for giving up the baby in the first place. She'd been twenty-seven, had no idea when she'd see J.D. again after that first time, and she'd just taken over the shelter.

It wasn't, she'd told herself, time to have a child. Particularly alone. She worked in the shelter, she knew how hard single parenting could be. And she wasn't tough enough, or brave enough, to take it on. No way.

But she'd left that letter in her file for a reason. And that reason was right here. Right now.

The last of the fog evaporated and Sam was filled with curiosity and, now that the surprise was abating, there was a bright shining chunk of happy at the center of her body. Happy that Spence and Jennifer were here. That this opportunity had walked in her door.

When she'd left the letter in her file with the adoption agency, she'd hoped this would happen. Had longed for a connection to her child, even if it wasn't as his mother.

A chance to know her son.

"No." Sam stood on trembling legs. "Please stay."

"Why?" Jennifer asked point-blank. "You don't appear interested or excited in any fashion. You seem ill. And I won't subject my son to you unless you are a hundred-percent interested in this meeting."

"I am," Sam said, trying to sound genuine. Trying to sound anything but totally freaked out. But it was hard. She was totally freaked out.

"You'll pardon me if I say, bullshit."

Sam laughed, incredulous. The woman even swore with manners. How funny that her son would end up with a woman so unlike her. So her opposite.

"Let me assure you," Jennifer said, her eyes shooting sparks, "from where I stand there is nothing funny about this situation."

Sam rocked back on her heels. She'd been knocked around a bit today and she found she'd hit her limit. "I'm sorry, Jennifer, if my reaction to you arriving on my doorstep without the courtesy of a phone call to prepare me isn't what you expected."

Jennifer's gaze fell to the floor.

"I've been in social services my whole working life and I know there is a protocol that is supposed to be followed—"

"I know," Jennifer said, not quite so righteous anymore. "I'm sorry. Spence has always known he was adopted and that his birth—" she glanced at Sam "—you were interested in meeting him. We'd promised that, when he was ready, if he was ever ready, we'd take the steps to find you. We had your address from the agency. I just—" She sighed and rubbed a hand down the buttons of her shirt. "I just never thought you'd still be here. I mean, who stays in the same place for nine years?"

"I do," Sam answered. "This is my home."

Jennifer's eyes widened in surprise. Her thoughts were so clearly broadcasted across her tight, pinched face that she might as well have just yelled "oh, dear God, you live in a woman's shelter," into a bullhorn.

"I run Serenity House," Sam said, trying not to get angry with the woman. "And I have for ten years. It was part of the reason I decided on adoption."

Jennifer licked her lips, staring at the floor as if for answers, or maybe cracks to fall into. But finally she heaved a big sigh and looked up, level and square, right into Sam's eyes. "Okay. I'm sorry, you're right. Arriving out of the blue was not fair. I'm not—" Jennifer stopped and for some reason Sam found herself holding her breath, wondering if the Ice Queen was about to crack. "I'm not thinking clearly lately. I'm sorry."

Well, Sam thought, that's much more civilized.

"I'm sorry, too, Jennifer, if my reaction indicated that I'm not totally thrilled you are here. I am. Please, sit," Sam said, urging the woman back into her chair. "I'm just a bit stunned."

Jennifer's careful smile didn't quite hide the palpable dislike she clearly felt, but after a moment, she sat, holding her sleek black bag on her lap like a shield.

"Now, perhaps we could begin again," Sam said, folding her hands in her lap, fighting the urge to go after her nails like they were dinner. "Perhaps you could tell me a little about Spence. About what he is expecting from this meeting." *Please, give me some kind of road map for this new place I'm in.*

My son, she thought, again, this time with a warmth running through her. Wow.

"Sure," Jennifer said and was silent, as if she didn't know where to start. "He has a lot of questions for you, in a notebook he keeps with him."

Okay, Sam thought. *Questions are good. I can answer questions.*

"He's rather intense about it," Jennifer said in a way that made Sam think that the description might not actually cover it.

"Intense?" she asked, slightly incredulous. He was nine after all.

Jennifer's entire body went rigid, her green eyes on fire. "Protocol or no, let me warn you, Sam. If, at any point, my son's feeling are in danger of being hurt, or you begin to disappoint him, we will leave. We've had enough heartache."

"Absolutely." Sam was quick to agree. Perhaps the incredulity needed to be put on hold. She understood the woman's baseline anxiety. It had to be fairly common among adoptive mothers when meeting birth mothers. "I have no intention of hurting him. If he's come to meet me, I would like to meet him."

Jennifer's gaze was like an X-ray sliding right through

Sam, photographing everything, but paying special attention to those faults, the flaws she couldn't hide. The black circles under her eyes, the messy hair, the nails bitten to the quick—a habit she couldn't seem to break. Nothing escaped Jennifer's cataloging gaze.

But Sam was seeing flaws in Jennifer, too. The woman was wound so tight she was about to crack. All that careful physical perfection was hiding something bad. Since most of the women who came through Serenity's doors had hit rock bottom, Sam recognized the signs.

This woman was pretending rock bottom wasn't rushing up to meet her.

Jennifer finally nodded. "I'll go get him," she said and ducked out the office door to the kitchen, where Spence sat at the table, a chocolate doughnut on a piece of paper towel in front of him.

Sam avoided Deb's curious eye and watched, with held breath, the interaction between Spence and Jennifer. The way he lit up at the sight of her, the way she leaned in, cupping the back of his head with her hand while she whispered in his ear.

His smile was a revelation and when he lifted his gaze to meet Sam's across the kitchen, she sucked in an astonished breath.

The crooked grin, the blue-gray eyes—he was J.D. in miniature.

Our son. A heaviness that felt something like grief settled into her bones. *The product of us.* The cause of that scar on her abdomen.

She'd thought one day she'd tell J.D. They'd talk about it like adults. Like the lovers they were. She never imagined him finding out this way. Not after the things he'd said to her this morning.

Considering the fight they'd just had, Sam was sure J.D. was packing right now and would be out the door in no time. He didn't have to know. He could go right on living his life without this knowledge.

And yes, that was convenient for her. And cowardly. But not telling him had become another habit she didn't know how to break.

So, she would respect the boy standing in the kitchen, the woman who had brought him—and she'd keep cold, cold J. D. Kronos away from both of them.

"Come on in," she said, waving Spencer and Jennifer into the privacy of her office all while listening for the creak of J.D.'s footsteps upstairs.

"Hi," Spencer said, coming to stand in front of her, the doughnut and paper towel in his hand. He tilted his head in the way J.D. did when he was thinking. His wary gaze met hers and she didn't read much excitement to see her. This was not the average nine-year-old, she realized. What had happened to this boy and his mother to make them so fragile? "You're Sam Riggins?"

"I am," she said, around a thick lump of emotion. "You're Spence Stern?"

"Spencer," he said. "My real name is Spencer but my mom calls me Spence."

"Well," Sam said with a smile. "My real name is Samantha but everyone calls me Sam."

Spence smiled and its effect was nothing less than the sun coming out from behind clouds. Sam felt some of the weight lift from her shoulders. No matter what might stem from this strange alignment of mother, father and child passing through each others' orbits, she was happy this boy was here.

"It's good to meet you," she said and stuck out her hand. "I've wondered about you for a long time."

Spence transferred his doughnut to the other hand and slipped his tiny palm into hers. "Likewise, Sam," he said, a smile on his lips, a fledgling twinkle in his eyes that was pure J. D. Kronos. But as soon as the twinkle was there, it was gone. And the intense boy-man was back. "Now, I've got some questions."

Jennifer smiled, stroking her son's hair, then turned to give Sam an assessing glare before walking past her into the office.

Sam leaned out into the kitchen toward Deb.

"You're good here?" She asked.

"Of course," Deb said.

"I'll just be in my office," she said.

"What about J.D.?" Deb said, her face revealing nothing and Sam had a wild jolt of fear that Deb had seen the resemblance between the man upstairs and the kid in her office.

"What about him?"

"Well, he's bound to come downstairs at some point and ask about you."

"Knock on the office door if he does," she said. "But you do it, not him."

"What's going on here, Sam?"

"Nothing. I mean..." She sighed. Working in this business had taught her the difference between a good lie and a stinker—and a little bit of truth was always the difference. "We got in a fight this morning," she said. "And I'm not ready to see him."

Deb clucked her tongue and shook her head. "You're not being honest about something, Sam," she said. "I'm no fool and neither is that man upstairs."

"I'll explain everything. Just...not now."

"Fine. I'll knock if he comes down."

Relieved, she ducked into her office and shut the door firmly behind her, hoping it was enough to keep the out-of-control portions of her life from mixing.

5

Sam Riggins was really tall. Way taller than Mom, Spence thought, watching the two women try to figure out where to sit and which way to cross their legs so they didn't hit each other.

My moms.

Thinking that made him happy. Looking at them, even though they were so totally different, seemed right, like when he got a perfect on his spelling test.

He pulled his Minecraft notebook out of his backpack and hoped he'd thought of everything. He'd tried to be thorough. Dad had helped as much as he could until they put the tubes in that made it impossible for him to talk.

After that the nurses at the hospital had been really nice and gave Spence some forms from the emergency room to copy.

Toward the end, everyone at the hospital did pretty much whatever Spence had asked.

Which was nice in a totally sucky way.

"So?" Sam finally said, smiling at him. It wasn't a fake smile, which was cool. He was really sick of the fake smiles people gave him, like he didn't know they were pretending. They'd all been pretending, nonstop for, like, a year.

But Sam wasn't pretending, not with that smile.

"Spence, your mom tells me you have some questions."

He nodded, gripping his notebook, suddenly nervous.

This is it, he thought. *No playing around.*

His dad always told him that when you asked a question, you had to be ready for the answer—you had to be ready for the good and the bad. That was the nature of asking questions, he'd said.

Dad had been a lawyer and he asked a lot of questions. So he knew.

Dad always knew.

Dad, he wanted to cry, *why aren't you here? Why aren't you helping me?* He'd told Spence to do this, helped him think of the questions. But without his dad, Spence didn't know how to get to the bottom of things. Or why he should bother. Dad was gone. There wasn't much point to anything.

Missing Dad was like another backpack he carried with him everywhere. It was heavy and it hurt and sometimes he could barely stand it. Like right now.

"Spence?" Mom asked, rubbing his back, as if she knew. "Are you all right?"

He nodded, and quickly opened his notebook, finding the questions in the back.

"What's your blood type?" he asked and Sam blinked at him, looking like an owl.

"A positive," she finally said and smiled. "What's yours?"

"B negative." He wrote the answer down in his notebook, a little zing of excitement went through him. He felt like a detective. "So my other dad must have my blood, right?" he asked and turned to his mom, who looked so sad and angry. That's how she looked whenever he mentioned his mom and dad who weren't her and Doug. He didn't know what else to call them, though. Mom One? Mom Two? Birth Dad? Adopted Dad? Like that was going to happen?

"That's how that works? Right?" he asked. "I had to get my blood type from someone."

Mom nodded. "Sometimes. But it's no guarantee. Without knowing who your—"

"Spence," Sam interjected and he and his mom turned to look at her.

Whoa, he thought. *That's not a happy face.*

"I can't answer any questions about your dad."

"Doug Stern was his dad," Jennifer said, through tight lips.

"Right," Sam said carefully.

Spence held his breath, wondering if Mom was going to totally lose it. She looked like it. She looked like she was just a few steps away from a nuclear meltdown.

"I'm sorry. But I can't tell you anything about your birth father," Sam said.

He almost asked why. 'Cause, if anyone knew his birth father, it had to be Sam, right? But there was something in her face, like a big stop sign, that made him bite his tongue.

Maybe we'll try that later, he thought. And looked back down at his notebook.

"Do you have a history of cancer in your family?" he asked.

Sam and Mom shared a look. A look he understood well. A look that said, what's the weirdo doing? He got that look a lot at school. And it made him want to disappear.

Right now it made him want to put the notebook away and leave. Just run as far away from this place as possible. But he heard Dad's voice in his ear, telling him that important things were hard things, that's why they were important.

"What about heart problems?" he asked, when Sam didn't say anything. "Diabetes?"

"Spence?" Mom asked. "What are you doing?"

"Asking questions," he answered. Duh.

"But why—" Mom's eyes opened wide and filled with tears.

"Don't cry," he whispered but the tears only got bigger, like they were going to fall right out of her eyes and he couldn't take it. He didn't want to make her cry. He didn't want anyone else to hurt. He just wanted to do what Dad asked him to do. "Don't. I'm sorry. I won't ask these questions if it's going to make you cry." Dad was dead. He wouldn't know that Spence had given up before getting the answers.

Spence had just gotten Mom to get out of bed so they could go on this road trip. He'd gotten her to comb her hair and get dressed, so he didn't want her to go back to lying in bed, staring at the ceiling.

Then Mom smiled, though the tears were still there, and she pulled him into her arms. "Honey," she whispered in his ear. "Why are you asking these questions? You're not sick."

"Sick?" Sam asked.

Spence looked over at her. He had her red hair. If she had cancer or heart problems like Dad, he could have those, too. That's how it worked sometimes. Dad had died of the same thing his dad had died of, which was the same thing his brother had died of.

"But I could get sick," he said. "Any minute. All of us could. I need to know this stuff."

"Are all your questions about my medical history?" Sam asked, shaking her head, like she just didn't get it.

"No." He sort of lied. He had some other ones. But he wasn't ready to ask those.

Mom and Sam stared at him, just watched him until he started to feel sick. "Is this weird?" he whispered, hating the way he felt right now, like his skin was too tight and his mom and Sam thought he was a dork. "Dad told me I should do this. He helped me."

Mom's face went white and she wiped away at the tears under her eyes. "Helped you with what?" she whispered.

"With the questions. He told me I needed to know this. I do, right?"

Mom's face looked like it was going to break. "Oh, honey—"

"Yes," Sam said definitively. She reached out and squeezed his shoulder and Spence felt his mother tense. But he didn't know what he was supposed to do about any of it. Mom crying. Dad dying. Sam touching him.

He felt like he was going to throw up.

"Yes, you should know whatever you want," Sam said and sat back, her brown eyes nice and steady. He liked that about her. He couldn't handle any more sadness. Any more silence in his house. Any more sitting around and waiting for his dad to come back when he was dead. So he looked into those eyes that were all business.

"Are you ready?" she asked, sounding like one of the doctors at the hospital and he felt himself nod, relieved that she was taking this over.

It made his skin loosen and his stomach relax. "Ready," he said.

"My grandmother had diabetes," she said. "But she lived with it until she was seventy-two. No cancer as far as I know. I had a great-uncle who died of a heart attack but he was also about three hundred pounds and ate fried chicken like four times a week. My grandmother on my father's side...."

Spence bent over his notebook and wrote as fast as he could.

SAM SEARCHED her brain for any more medical history that she knew of, and figured she'd covered it all. Her folks were still alive and kicking in a condo in Florida. She had a cousin alive and producing babies at an alarming rate up in the Catskill Mountains.

But she wished she had more to give him, because the more she'd talked the more relaxed he'd gotten. But she'd hit the end of her line.

"All in all," she said, smiling at Spence, "you come from pretty hardy people."

Spence flipped a page on his notebook and Sam spared a glance at Jennifer, who had sat still and silent as a statue for the past twenty minutes. Staring at her son, as if she could soak him up through her eyes.

Sam didn't know the finer points of what had happened to these two, but she could fill in most of the blanks. And it made her want to put down her head and howl.

Clearly, Jennifer's husband, Spence's father, had died after a long, drawn-out battle against something, in a hospital. With lots of doctors. And lots of machines. And lots of medical history questions.

Poor Spence, she thought, watching the boy write frantically, his tongue peeking out between his teeth as he concentrated.

Every once in a while when she got particularly lonely—usually after J.D. left and she was alone in her apartment, feeling every minute of her age, and every repercussion of her commitment to the shelter—she thought of the boy she'd given up for adoption.

She thought of what he'd look like. What he would be interested in. She wondered if he was left-handed like her. If he slept on his stomach like J.D.

And looking at him, now, standing not two feet from her, she realized Spence in reality was better than anything she could have imagined. His hair was damp at the temples from sweat induced by the cramped quarters. His eyes, as he watched his mother, were so solemn, so careful. So aware of what Jennifer might be feeling.

"Do you have any more questions?" Sam asked.

"Not right now," he said, not meeting her eyes.

"Spence," Jennifer said. "We're not staying so if you have more quest—"

"What?" Spence asked. "What do you mean we're not staying?"

Jennifer glanced at Sam, clearly uncomfortable. But Sam was pretty uncomfortable, too. She wanted to add her protests to Spence's. Sam just met Spence. He'd just gotten here; they couldn't go so soon.

"We're not staying," Jennifer said, the Ice Queen once again. "We have to go home."

"But we just got here, Mom."

"There aren't any hotels—"

"You can stay here," Sam said, ignoring the peeved look Jennifer sent her way. "We have plenty of room."

"Here?" Jennifer asked, the irritation on her face turning to horror.

"Yes," Sam said. The thought of J.D. entered her mind, but she pushed him away. If he was still here, she could deal with him later. She wanted the boy to stay. "I assure you, the rooms are clean and you'd have plenty of privacy."

"Mom," Spence said and laid his hand on Jennifer's leg. "Please. I'd like to stay. For a few days."

Jennifer took a deep breath that shuddered audibly at the top, as though she was fighting tears or screams or some other powerful response. Sam felt bad for the woman—she really did—but Sam was fighting, too. For something she wanted.

A chance to know her son.

"A few days," Sam said, nodding her head in total agreement. "Maybe just for the weekend."

It was a long, frozen moment before Jennifer finally conceded and Sam and Spence both let out big sighs of relief then turned and smiled at each other.

Connection buzzed between them, and all the hair on her arms stood at attention. A wave of something big, something strong and grateful rolled through her.

This was good.

She wanted to reach out for the boy, touch one of the ginger curls that twisted near his ear. She wanted to pat his shoulder, feel the small bones beneath his skin and know that part of her was in him.

"I'm so glad you're here," she said to him.

"Deb." J.D.'s voice filtered through the office, muffled by the door. Sam's heart chugged, her blood turning to sludge. "My computer is in the office. I'm just going—"

The door cracked open and Sam leaped to her feet, but it was too late. The door opened all the way.

"J.D.," she said sharply, trying to step in front of Spence, but the kid ducked around, watching J.D. as he entered the office, a big black shadow in blue jeans and a gray shirt.

Now that J.D. was in the same room with Spencer, she

saw that they shared so much more than eye color and smiles. Spencer had the same square shape to his face, the long eyelashes and thick eyebrows.

Outside of the red hair, he was all J.D.

"Oh." He paused when he saw Jennifer. "Sorry." His crooked smile was brief, warm, the bigger version of Spence's and Jennifer sat up straight at the sight of it, her hand over her heart.

She knew, Sam thought. Oh, God. She knew.

"Deb didn't say you were with anyone," J.D. explained.

"You should go," Sam snapped. She was on thin, thin ice and it was cracking under her feet. Every moment Spence and J.D. were in the same room was a moment closer to reckoning. And she couldn't do it. She wasn't strong enough. Tough enough to handle J.D.'s rage on top of all that had happened today.

"Okay." J.D.'s brow furrowed at the tone of her voice. "Can you hand me—"

She grabbed his laptop even as he talked and she thrust it into his hands.

"Thanks. Sorry, again." He nodded to Jennifer then seemed to, for the first time, see Spence standing so still, a tiny statue beside his mother.

Sam held her breath and prayed.

"Hi," Spence said into the vast silence.

"Hi," J.D. answered, his voice like sandpaper over Sam's exposed nerves. J.D's eyes, identical to Spence's, looked at the boy, took in everything—the red hair, the distinctive eyes, the quirky smile—and Sam felt her bones melt, just disappear, leaving her without support. Without strength.

Finally, J.D. turned to her, his eyes on her stomach. On the scar that he couldn't see but knew was there and she lifted her hands to it, felt the ridge under the thin cotton of her shirt. Felt it pulse under her fingertips like a guilty secret.

He knows, she thought. *This is it. He knows.*

J.D.'s gaze lifted to hers and she braced herself for the rage. The fierce and totally warranted anger that would eviscerate her, totally gut her.

But his eyes were blank. Empty. His face expressionless. He waited, watching her, like she was a stranger he needed something from and she found herself nodding. One small dip of her chin.

Yes, the nod said. *He's ours.*

And then, as if he'd never been there, J.D. left.

J.D. DIDN'T BOTHER PUTTING his laptop in the soft briefcase. He just tucked the machine under his arm, grabbed his bags and headed for his car.

Never once looking back.

He didn't think of her. He definitely didn't think of the kid. He thought of the fastest route home, to his empty house in Newark. He thought of construction on the Beltway and of maybe stopping in Baltimore.

All the skin he shed in order to be the man he was here he pulled back on, inch by painful inch. He piled on his past, his crimes, his genetics and secrets until the man who stayed at Serenity was nowhere to be found.

And he couldn't believe how much that sucked.

"J.D." Her voice behind him, panting and panicked, was like a stick of dynamite against the dam he erected to keep his reaction to what had just been revealed from flattening him.

So he kept walking. Faster.

The sun was out now, but clouds gathered over the distant ocean to the east, which would make traffic a bitch.

He heard her running, her pounding feet catching up to him and he felt something like anger build like a brush fire in his bloodstream.

"J.D.," she cried. "Stop. Please. I want to—" She touched him. The warm, damp flesh of her palm against the skin of his arm.

And the dam broke.

He tossed his bags, the computer, his car keys onto the asphalt of the parking lot and turned on her. He couldn't catalog what he felt. He couldn't put names to the pain and anger and betrayal that choked him. That sucked the air from his body. The thoughts from his head.

But it must have been on his face because Sam had the good sense to look scared.

To look terrified.

He hated that. He hated the white tension around her lips, the widening of her eyes. He'd spent so many years trying to make sure she was never scared of him. That she never saw the worst in him, what he was capable of. But he couldn't control himself right now.

He was turning into the monster he always tried to hide from her.

She backed up a step, walking away from him.

"My son?" he said, stalking her.

"Y-yes," she stuttered, coming to stop against her own car in the parking space closest to the shelter. "Yes. He's ours." She didn't look away, but met his eyes and his anger head-on and it made him angrier. Where was her shame? For crying out loud? This woman whom he'd admired and respected for so long, this woman he'd moved heaven and earth for in ways she'd never, ever know, who, in his own warped way, he'd loved. Loved to the best of his ability.

And right now he wanted to rub her nose in this mess. Punish her.

He understood suddenly, how all those clients he pitied felt when he told them the truths they were so afraid of.

"When?" He didn't stop until he was a breath away from her.

"Nine." She licked her lips. "Nine years ago."

"What?" he asked, shocked. The memory of the first time they made love sizzled in his brain. He'd been so taken by her when he'd first met her. So intrigued. So half in love that when they'd touched in the darkness of her office, by accident, he'd kissed her.

And she'd kissed him back.

There was no way she'd—

"I, ah...got pregnant. The...the first time. In the office."

His chest worked like a bellows and he could barely suck in enough oxygen to keep his mind from shorting out with anger. She'd kept his son a secret for nine years?

"Why?" he asked.

"Why, what?"

"Did you lie?" he whispered.

"I didn't lie," she said and her eyelids twitched. "I just didn't tell you."

He shook his head. "Coward," he spat, and turned away. He couldn't talk to her if she was going to play games.

"Yes," she said, jumping in front of him, her strong body a tall, thin barricade between him and his car. "I'm sorry," she said. "I am. I should have told you. I mean't to, I can't even tell you how many times I meant to tell you."

One of the first lessons his uncle Milo taught him was that everyone lied. Everyone. And J.D. had believed him. But when he'd met Sam he'd actually thought she was the exception. He'd never thought her capable of lying, but she was doing it right now.

"Out of my way, Sam," he said, picking up his stuff.

"I want to talk to you about this."

"No." He glared at her. "You want to lie to me about this. You want to make yourself feel better about what you've done."

Her face was white, her bones standing out under the porcelain of her skin. Anger and guilt rolled off her in waves.

"What should I have done, J.D.?" she whispered. "You left the next morning without saying a word to me and I didn't hear from you for a year."

"You didn't call me, either." Not to tell him she was pregnant. Not to tell him she needed his help. Nothing.

"I told myself I would tell you if you called. If you came through town, I'd confess all. But you didn't."

"What about when I did come back?" he asked. "Why didn't you tell me?"

"Because it was over," she said. "I'd made my decision. And it was my decision. My body. It just didn't make sense-"

"*Didn't make sense?*" He refused to feel bad about the way he'd left after that first time. The way he'd forced himself not to call her, or see her. The way he'd buried himself in work so he couldn't remember the sweet silk of her body.

"I thought it was a one-night stand," she cried. "I never thought I'd see you again. What would have been the point?"

The point? He wanted to howl. *The point is my son! A boy I didn't know about.* But if he said that, if those words came out of his mouth, he didn't know what else would come out.

"What would have happened if I told you I was pregnant?" She asked.

"That's not fair."

"None of this is fair. We were strangers. Would you have wanted a kid? A family?"

A kid. God. He'd never dreamed of having a child. He never thought he'd ever get close enough to someone to risk a baby. Sam had been the closest and he'd made sure they always were protected. Fat lot of good that did.

A flash of something, like a scene from a movie, or part of a dream that he didn't quite remember, cut through his anger like a spotlight.

The three of them—him, Sam and the boy—around a table laden with food and Sam's laughter.

A family.

And just as quickly he remembered his own family. The missing mother, the drunk father. The blood and tears.

That was what he knew about family. That's the legacy he had for the boy and he didn't want to give that to anyone.

"No," he said and he watched her exhale like she'd been holding her breath. "But that doesn't change the fact that you should have told me."

"I know," she whispered. "And I'm sorry.

Quickly, because his sanity depended on it, he hoisted his duffel bag onto his shoulder and muscled his way past her.

"What are you doing?"

"Leaving," he said, turning, briefly, one last time to see her. To memorize the curves of her face, the sun in her hair, the lies in her eyes. "I'll send you the name of a good PI. Don't call me again, Sam."

6

J.D. could compartmentalize with the best of them. Drug lords, sociopaths, murderers—they had nothing on J.D.'s ability to take the horrors of his life, the things he'd seen and done, and prevent them from bleeding into his daily existence.

He could sleep like a baby after providing information that broke up a marriage.

He could make breakfast after sending a guy to the hospital.

He could look himself in the mirror after delivering a guy to a crime boss, effectively signing the man's death warrant.

He could be a monster in the real world...and a different man at Serenity House.

It was a gift from his father, along with the color of his eyes and a temper like a powder keg.

The boy had J.D.'s eyes. The color was identical to his, to his father's, to his grandfather's. J.D. could only hope the boy didn't get the temper that seemed to go with it.

Please, he thought, his stomach churning, *don't let him be like us. Let that kid be different.*

Then, because he had to, he folded up the pain and the betrayal that Sam had served him on a silver platter and he shoved them deep into his head.

He locked them up tight with memories of dear old Dad and he drove carefully, obeying all traffic laws, toward the interstate.

It would take a while, he knew, to forget her. To forget the living, breathing nine-year-old piece of himself that was out in the world. To forget the man he'd been at Serenity House, the peace he'd found there. But he could do it.

Years of practice had helped him wipe out the memory of his father's face, the smell of his own blood and the sound of metal bars slamming home behind him.

He knew it took time, and good solid locks on those memories he kept tucked away.

But right now, despite his steady foot on the gas, his hands shook. And sweat ran down the back of his neck in a cold annoying trickle.

Sam, he thought before he could stop himself. *How could you do this?*

The sound of his cell phone ringing cut through the silence of his car. Grateful for the distraction, he dug it out of the front pocket of his briefcase.

The number on the display was not Sam's—not that he expected her to call—so he flipped it open.

"Jakos? Did you get my e-mail?" Greg Spili wasted no time with pleasantries, one of the very few reasons J.D. was still friends with the guy despite the fact that he called J.D. by his birth name, which was a huge pain in the ass.

"No," J.D. said, wincing slightly. The Jane Doe situation.

He'd totally forgotten. "I haven't looked at my computer this morning. What's happening?"

"It's Christina Conti all right," Greg said. "And we've got a situation."

"Who's we?" J.D. asked, a yawning pit opening in his stomach. "You and me? Or you and Uncle Sam?"

"You, me, Uncle Sam and whoever this friend of yours is who has her."

J.D. shut his eyes briefly and swore without making a sound. He'd been afraid of this. And in the commotion of the morning he'd forgotten all about the very real threat bearing down on Sam and Serenity House.

Francis Conti. Crap.

"How big of a situation?" he asked. "Is Conti after Christina?"

"Not yet," Greg said. "He still thinks Christina is visiting her sister at NYU. But the boyfriend has agreed to come in tonight."

"For what?"

"For dinner, you ass. What do you think? He's got information on Conti."

J.D. pulled over to the side of the road before asking his question. "How does this involve me? Or my friend."

"Are you being stupid on purpose?" Greg asked. "Because once this boy is off the streets, Conti is going to put two and two together, get five and come looking for Christina."

That's what J.D. had been afraid of, but the good times they didn't stop rolling.

"And we need her," Greg added. "We need Christina to stay put because once this boyfriend talks, we might be able to leverage her into talking, too. And we can't do that if she runs again."

"I can't stop that," J.D. said, wanting to fight the inevitable for as long as he could.

"No, you *won't* stop it. It's a choice. I've been telling you for years, that you've made your—"

"Weren't we talking about the mob?" J.D. asked, grinding his teeth.

"Look, Jakos, if you won't do it for the good of the girl, or for the United States government, or me..." He paused and J.D. didn't say anything. Greg always put too much stock in their past. This friendship that Greg relentlessly held on to.

Greg sighed. "Do it for this friend of yours. This friend who found Christina. Because if Conti tracks his daughter to wherever your friend is, things are going to go real bad, real fast."

Crap.

That's what J.D. had been afraid of.

He couldn't let Sam twist in the wind like this. Not with Conti threatening like a hurricane. No matter how much he hated her right now—and he did, he truly did—he didn't hate her enough to want to see her dead. Or hurt.

J.D. checked his mirrors and pulled a U-turn, heading back to the shelter.

"This friend wouldn't happen to be that woman, would it?" Greg asked. "The woman that runs the shelter? That you—"

"What's the time frame?" J.D. interrupted. One night of too much ouzo with Greg and the bastard had all his secrets. His skin felt two sizes too small and he wanted to put his fist through something. Anything. Greg, preferably.

Greg sighed, but got back on task. "Boyfriend is coming in tonight. I can call you tomorrow morning. You should be off babysitting duty by the end of the weekend."

J.D. hung up without saying anything else and tossed his phone onto the passenger seat. Babysitting.

Those compartments he kept all the messy details of his life in threatened to split, as his heart pounded hard against his chest, his rib cage getting battered with every surge of his blood.

He was going back to Sam. Christ, even after everything that happened, she was a magnet he couldn't run from. But he wasn't going back as the man she knew. That J.D. was gone. She'd come face-to-face with everything he'd tried to protect her from.

And the boy was there. The boy with his eyes and Sam's hair.

Curiosity, a bittersweet regret, welled up like tar, like poisonous gas. What was he like? J.D. wondered but then he squelched the desire to know.

The boy, like Sam, was nothing. J.D. had a job. A time frame and that was it.

And he repeated that mantra until his hands stopped shaking.

"You sure you don't want to stay in our room?" Mom asked as Spence flopped down on one of the big comfy couches in the common area.

She looked around the room like there might be cockroaches in the bookshelves, or fleas on the two couches. He could tell she was just dying to coat the whole thing in that no-water soap stuff that she loved so much.

"Mom." He sighed. "It's cool."

"What is?" she asked, blinking at him. She just had no clue.

"Being here," he explained, twisting the wire of his notebook in the holes it was threaded through. He didn't look at her face because he didn't want to see how disappointed she was. "I like it here. It's nice."

Mom laughed and even though it was weak, Spence's stomach relaxed. It had been a long time since he'd heard that sound at all, and he had to think that this road trip had been the right thing to do. He got answers and she laughed.

"I wouldn't say nice, but it will do, I suppose." She eyed him hard. "For a few days. That's all. We can't stay—"

"I know," he told her, cutting off her lecture. But he didn't know what she was in such a rush to get back to. Bed? Not work, since she hadn't done that for six months. Their empty house? He hated the idea of going back there, with Dad's shoes by the door and his magazines in the bathroom, and his smell everywhere.

She sat next to him, on the very edge of the couch, like if she sat all the way back something might rub off on her. "I'm really proud of you," she said, stroking his hair, which he hated but he let her do it. "Have I told you that?"

Not recently. "Yep."

"And I love you. Your dad loved you."

Spence looked down at the miner on his note-book; he traced the edge of a green block with his thumb. "I know," he whispered past the huge ball in his throat.

"Okay." She sighed. "I'm going to go talk to Sam real quick and finish bringing in some stuff from the car. I need to make a few phone calls, too."

"I'll be fine, Mom," he assured her. He was dying to open his notebook. He wanted to read what he'd written and add a few more questions to his "ask Sam later" list. Mrs. Brown, his therapist, told him that when he had questions for his dad that he should write a letter to him, which was sort of lame, considering Dad was dead. But, right now, it sounded like a good thing to do. There was so much he wanted to tell Dad. And Spence didn't have any other way to do it.

Mom looked at him for a long time, something she'd been doing more and more of and it made him nervous. "Go, Mom," he told her, unable to stand it any longer. "I'll be fine."

Finally she left and Spence sighed, flopping sideways on the couch.

"You okay, kid?" someone asked and he shot up.

"Who said that?"

"Me." A skinny girl with dark hair stood up from behind the couch.

"Are you spying?" he asked. In the adult world, nothing was worse than spying. He'd gotten sent to his room more times than he could count for doing it. But he never realized what was wrong with it until right now.

His face felt hot and itchy when he thought of all the sappy things the girl must have heard.

"I didn't mean to," the girl said, leaning against the couch. "I was reading." She lifted the big book she was reading and he caught the title. *What to Expect When You're Expecting.*

Expecting what? he wondered. But then the girl stepped around the couch and he realized she was pregnant.

Following her was a giant black dog.

"Is that your dog?" he asked, pulling his feet up onto the couch in case the dog was hungry.

"No," she said, then awkwardly patted the dog on the top of its giant head. "But she follows me."

"Where?"

"Everywhere," the girl answered. The pats turned into scratches and the dog's mouth fell open. A giant tongue rolled out and the monster leaned against the girl. "She slept outside my door last night."

"She?" he asked.

"Daisy," the girl said. "Give her a pat. Don't worry, she only looks mean."

Right. Like Spence was going to believe that. But still he leaned across the couch, very carefully, and reached for the dog's head. Daisy darted away for a moment and Spence froze, terrified. But then Daisy leaned forward and sniffed his hand, the whole thing. His fingers, his wrist, his palm, then that giant tongue came back out and licked Spence's fingers.

"See?" the girl said, smiling a little. "She's nice."

Yeah, Spence thought, his heart beating like crazy. *Nice and scary.*

"You live here?" he asked. He'd never met a girl who lived in a shelter before. Why was she here? Why didn't she live with her mom? Or the guy who got her pregnant? Why were her hands all splotchy with dark stuff?

"I'm staying here for a while," she said, sitting on the far end of the couch. Daisy parked herself at the girl's feet.

"Me, too," he said. "Me and my mom."

She nodded, but watched him out of the side of her eyes, like she had a bunch of questions, too.

"I'm not *staying here*, staying here," he said, totally embarrassed because she was so pretty and still looking at him. "I mean, I have a home. That I live in. Usually."

"Me, too," she said, smiling. "Usually. I'm...ah... Jane."

"I'm Spence," he said. He wondered if he should reach out and shake her hand. That was what he was supposed to do when meeting a new person, but Jane didn't seem interested and he'd already looked like a big enough dork.

She turned a few pages in her book and he opened his

notebook, wondering if they were just going to sit here and read.

"So?" she asked, still flipping through pages of the book on her lap. "You okay?"

Yeah, jumped to his tongue, because that's the answer he'd been giving to every teacher and doctor and nurse for the past six months. *Yeah*, he'd say. *I'm fine. Yeah*, he'd say. *We're okay.*

He'd been lying each and every time and he wanted to stop. His father was dead. His mom was acting like a person he didn't even know.

And what was really freaking him out, was Sam had a distant cousin who had Parkinson's disease, and Spence wasn't sure what that was but he bet he had it.

So, no. He wasn't all right.

"Not really," he said and with the words a big weight that had been sitting on his chest, making it hard to breathe, was gone.

The girl smiled with half her mouth. "Me, neither."

Suddenly the front door opened with a wild bang and a man walked in, pausing slightly to look at Spence and the girl. He held a key in his hand.

It was the guy from earlier, the guy Sam had gone running after.

The guy with Spence's eyes and nose and eyebrows.

The girl next to him sucked in a quick breath and tensed like she was going to run. Not Spence. He couldn't have run if he had to. The guy was nailing him to the couch with those eyes. With his hard heavy look.

The guy flexed his jaw, like he was about to say something. He even opened his mouth, but then he shut it. Nodded real quick and left.

The girl sighed, her whole body relaxing into the brown couch. "Do you know that guy?" she asked.

Spence shook his head.

The girl whistled and shook her head. "He sure looks like you. I mean, those eyes, it's weird."

"Weird?" he whispered, thinking the exact same thing.

"He could…like…be your dad or something."

Sam was trying desperately to get her life back on the rails it had been utterly bounced off. It took superhuman effort not to go upstairs, medicate and crawl into bed. Start the whole day over tomorrow, pretend that none of this had happened.

Except Spence. She wasn't about to pretend he wasn't here. In fact, it was equally hard not to track him down and start asking some questions of her own. Are you happy? Do you like art? What happened to your dad? Why is your mother so cold and angry? Why does she hate me? Do you hate me?

All good questions, important questions. But Spence had looked as though he needed a break and Jennifer had looked about to break and Sam had a to-do list a mile long. So they'd all given each other some space.

The questions would have to wait. And her medicated vacation under her duvet would have to wait. Work was what was important right now. Work was always important.

She chewed on her thumbnail and looked down at a to-do list that used to make sense, but now seemed so removed from the present moment it was impossible to fathom when it was written, much less by whom.

Nowhere on the list did it mention getting to know her son. She'd also neglected to list "sleep with a stranger for ten years." And it never occurred to her to add "lie to yourself about that stranger about a million times a day."

Nope. Between calling the plumber, meeting with the accountant and interviewing day-care staff, she'd missed every important thing in her life.

How long had that been happening? How long had she been lost in the mayhem of running the shelter? She'd told Bob she didn't want a family. Didn't want a marriage, and she didn't. She knew that. It was part of why she'd given up the baby. But how much of that decision was something she accepted as a byproduct of throwing her entire life into the shelter? And how much was truly her heart's desire?

It was all so muddy right now. Confused. And her life wasn't like that.

Shaken and frustrated, she pushed the list away. There was no concentrating on anything.

She'd muscled all thoughts of J.D. as far away as possible. She'd watched his car drive away until the brake lights vanished and she'd felt her life change, right then. A chapter over. Time to turn the page, start over. Start something new. A relationship with her son.

No time to mourn what she'd had—or thought she'd had—with J.D. No chance to imagine what might have been between them without all the secrets. The lies.

But those thoughts kept sneaking up on her. Grief was knocking on her door. So she gave in.

Resting her head back on her chair, she just opened herself up to the pain and it crashed over her like a waterfall —never-ending, utterly disorienting, terrifying.

J.D., her whole body wanted to scream.

His reaction in the parking lot had been in line with

what she'd expected when he heard the news. Well, that wasn't true. His reaction in the parking lot was a million times worse. She'd expected anger. She'd expected blame. But she hadn't expected that he'd leave. Just walk away without giving her a chance to explain.

It hurt. It hurt so much that he could walk away like that. Like she didn't matter. Like Spence didn't matter. That ten years together were nothing.

In fact, combined with the revelation earlier—that she'd been sleeping with a man she clearly didn't know—she was totally adrift. She could barely figure out what was real and what was this new nightmare.

I don't even know who I am, she realized, staring down at her hands. *I lied to him. I kept the truth from him. I'm no better than him at all.*

Oh, man, that was the worst. It hurt to see herself that way. To know herself for what she really was. A coward.

But what did keeping secrets make J.D.? She started to answer that, then stopped herself. She'd made this mistake before, answering her own questions about him. Filling in the blanks of her knowledge with things she wanted to believe.

He was a hero.

A good guy.

A man to love.

Ha!

Were she any less destroyed by the events of the day, she'd laugh.

The only thing she knew for sure about J.D. was that she didn't know him at all. And now he was gone.

And that somehow hurt the most. Life without J.D.—without the J.D. she thought she knew, without fantasizing about that man, anticipating him, imagining him—was all such a bleak affair.

She had work, J.D. and thoughts of J.D. That was it. The sum total of her life. And she wished for one more chance to tell him she was sorry and that he was a jerk.

"Sam?"

For a moment she thought she'd created the sound of his voice, pulled him back here by sheer force of will and fantasy so they could get some closure on this chapter of her life.

But then she heard the soft click of her office door shutting and smelled the spicy scent of J.D. and her whole body reacted, tensed wildly in a sudden fight-or-flight instinct.

"What are you doing here?" she asked, turning to face him with what she hoped was a passable imitation of indifference.

"Your Jane Doe is trouble," he said, his face impenetrable. So cold it made her efforts at calculated nonchalance look like sobbing.

Right, Jane Doe. It seemed like a million years ago that girl walked into Serenity House.

"What's the story?" Sam asked, leaning back in her chair, happy to have something else to concentrate on. And as usual, the shelter provided plenty of reason for her to never have to think about herself or her life.

"Jane's name is Christina Conti. Her father is Francis Conti, a capo in the Gamboni crime family."

Sam's stomach fell through the floor. This was more than trouble. Way more than trouble.

This was Eve's death all over again.

"She's running from him?" she asked.

"Apparently." J.D. widened his legs and crossed his arms

over his chest, all business. All calm, cool and collected stranger.

She wished she could turn away from him, stop seeing him so the hurting in her chest could just be done.

But it wasn't possible. It had never been possible with him. If he was nearby, he drew her like the sun.

"Is he looking for her?" she asked.

"Not yet. Christina's story about visiting her sister is true. Frank is still buying it and hasn't bothered to call the sister. But it's only a matter of time."

"So what do we do?" she asked, her voice tight and scared. "What are we talking about here?"

"I know it sounds bad. But I don't think we need to worry about them showing up here just yet. I've got a friend in the bureau who is reaching out to Christina's boyfriend. Apparently, there's no love lost between him and Frank, particularly after learning that Christina was pregnant."

Ah, Sam thought, connecting the dots. The father was involved but not in an incestuous way. In an I'm-going-to-shoot-you-in-the-back-of-the-head-for-touching-my-daughter kind of way.

What a relief, Sam thought, the irony heartbreaking.

"So?" Sam asked. "What am I supposed to do with a pregnant mafia princess?"

"Keep her here," J.D. answered and Sam's eyebrows hit her hairline.

"You're kidding, right? Keep her here until when? Frank shows up with a machine gun?"

"No, until my friend shows up with the boyfriend."

Sam blinked, her knotted stomach making it hard for her to breathe. Wait until the boyfriend and the FBI agent showed up and pray that it was before Frank got smart and started following Christina's trail to here?

That was an ugly and potentially brutal waiting game.

"I know what you're thinking, Sam, and it's not that bad. Really. Frank doesn't know she's here and by the time he realizes his daughter has run away, this will all be over. And even if he does figure it out, it would take him days to trace her here."

"You're sure?" she asked. And she knew it was ludicrous to trust him, to need his assurances, but she did. She'd never trust him with her heart or her body again, but she could trust him in this. It was his job, after all, and he was very good at his job.

He nodded and she took some solace in that.

But after the day she'd had, her nerves of steel were fraying. And she knew she couldn't handle this alone. This was why J.D. was in the Rolodex.

But asking him for help now seemed like rubbing salt in her own emotional wounds. The words were stuck behind her pride and her own mistakes.

"You okay?" J.D. asked, and she hated his intuition. Hated the way he knew her.

"I'm pretty freaked out," she admitted. "I'd be lying if I told you otherwise."

"I really don't think it's going to turn into anything," he said.

"Well, not for you," she said. "You'll be back home in—"

"I'm staying, Sam," he interjected, his eyes momentarily familiar. Momentarily warm. "I won't leave you. Not until my friend shows up."

I won't leave you. The words were so beguiling.

Oh, but you have, J.D., she thought. *The J.D. I knew and loved has vanished and I don't know this replacement.*

"Okay," she said. Grateful, she hoped for the last time, that he was here when she needed him. "Thank you."

"Well," he muttered. "I'm sleeping on your couch so don't thank me yet."

She sucked in a quick breath. Of course he'd stay in her apartment. With Spence and Jennifer taking the last room, her couch was the only place to sleep.

"Funny, isn't it?" he asked, in a tone of voice that indicated he found nothing at all entertaining about this. "Twelve hours ago staying the weekend would have seemed like a dream come true."

She nodded, lanced with pain, imagining how the weekend could have been different. How just a few hours ago her whole life had been different.

"Spence and Jennifer are staying the weekend, too," she said.

"Who?"

"Your son."

He flinched as if she'd punched him. "Don't call him that," he said, his voice icy. "He doesn't ever need to know that I have anything to do with him."

"But," she murmured, "he's your son—"

He held up his hand, cutting off her words. "He doesn't need to know that," he said.

There were so many things to say. Details to get straight, questions to ask, truth to tell. She wanted to dig into him, sift through him with her fingers, find everything he hid from her like rocks buried in sand. Relentlessly she wanted to lay him open so she could see truly, who he was.

He must have wanted to do the same to her.

Maybe this could be a chance for them. To start over without the secrets. To show each other who they really were.

She opened her mouth to apologize and explain again

but he shook his head, his eyes piercing her skin, seeing her intentions, her anger and grief.

"It won't change anything," he said. "I'll be gone on Monday and until then, nothing's personal."

He left without another word.

7

The kid was following him. The kid and Daisy, actually. From the parking lot, through the side yard, around the back of the shelter.

J.D. could not believe it, but the sound of the boy following him through the grass and kudzu vines as he circled the house, checking locks, could not be mistaken.

A hot wind blew through the trees, bringing the smell of the kid that chilled him to the bone, despite the heat of the day.

My son smells like doughnuts and pencil graphite.

Uncle Milo would advise J.D. to trap the kid. To turn and confront him. Scare the bejesus out of the boy so he'd leave him alone. Actually, only if the boy wasn't his son. As his son, Uncle Milo would no doubt have a totally different piece of advice.

Talk to the boy, he'd say. *Get to know your flesh and blood. Give him some answers.*

But since that was definitely not going to happen and J.D. had had enough of confrontations, and Uncle Milo had been dead for ten years, J.D. veered off toward the thin woods to the left of the shelter that had a few trails and a small swimming pond at the center of it, hoping to force the kid to lose interest but it didn't work.

The boy followed. And Daisy followed the boy.

God. The kid needed a lesson in the dangers of strangers. What nine-year-old followed a man he didn't know into the woods?

"Are you looking for trouble?" J.D. asked. The kid was so startled he dropped his notebook and frantically reached down to grab it.

Daisy growled at J.D. and he shot the dog a can-it glare. The last thing he needed was Daisy thinking he was the bad guy, too.

"No, ah...I'm not. I'm looking for you."

Same thing, J.D. wanted to say. "Well, your mom should have taught you not to follow strangers into the woods."

"She did. I mean...she taught me stuff like that... about strangers. Not about the woods, specifically." For one wild brave moment the kid looked him square in the eye and J.D. felt a pulse, a giant tug on his guts.

The kid went back to studying his notebook and with those eyes off him, J.D. could breathe again. "Go away."

"I wanted to ask you some questions." The boy didn't move, but he didn't look up either.

J.D. ignored him, turned and walked farther into the woods, wiping away the sweat rolling off his forehead and swatting at mosquitoes. For a moment it seemed as though the kid had gotten the message. Then the sound of breaking twigs and rustling leaves followed him.

"I'm not kidding, boy," he growled. "Go. Away."

The kid was terrified and for the scarcest moments J.D. felt a small breath of guilt, against the nape of his neck, but he dismissed it. There was no point in catering to this kid.

No point in answering his questions, or spending time with him.

Even his uncle's voice, reminding him that there wasn't any virtue in cruelty, couldn't stop him.

J.D. walked past the boy toward the shelter, careful not to get too close to Spence's ginger curls or fresh pencil smell.

There was work to be done and he felt the old suction of Serenity House. Sam's J.D. looked around and saw ways to help, ways to make things easier on Sam and the women here.

J. D. Kronos, private investigator, saw a million weaknesses.

First things first. He had to replace a lock on the kitchen window. He didn't think Francis was going to show up—J.D. could put a little faith in Greg and the U.S. government—but Sam should know better than to leave the broken lock that was there on the window.

There was a drainpipe, so easily climbable it was stupid, that marched right up the side of the house past Sam's bedroom window.

The kudzu vines were creeping across the rear of the yard and needed to be chopped back to the tree line, something Sam usually did with regularity, but maybe she'd been too busy.

The pipe under the sink was no doubt leaking again. He could take another look at that.

Odd, to do such things for her, the things he used to like doing for her, when just thinking about her made his head pound.

Above all, he had to avoid Sam. Avoid her apartment where it seemed everywhere he turned held some kind of X-rated memory. And if that meant repainting the damn shelter, he'd do it.

"Do you have B negative blood?" Spencer asked, persistent as all get-out.

"Why?" he asked, facing the kid, who was blushing so hard it was amazing the trees next to him didn't go up in flames.

"Just wondering."

"About my blood type?"

"Science experiment."

J.D. almost laughed. As lies went, it was pretty good. But not good enough to make him stay or to answer the question.

"Are you Jonathon David Kronos?" Spencer asked, his blush building and turning him nearly purple.

J.D. wanted to take pity on the kid. He really did. But Sam didn't know his real name. He'd made sure of it.

"Nope," he answered, in all honesty. And this time when he walked away the kid didn't say anything.

SAM LIKED dinnertime at the shelter the best. It reminded her of growing up with her own family in Texas. And since she was emotionally close to her family—although geographically distant—dinner hour at Serenity made her believe that the women she helped and the friends she worked with were family enough for anyone.

There was laughter. Homework. Communal cooking. Talk about the day and its success and failures.

Tonight was a small group, but merry.

Even Christina sat at the table, breaking lettuce into chunks, watching the meal preparation with wide eyes. Deb sat next to her. Shonny, Deb's little boy, played on the oak floor beside them.

Dinnertime was female and it was tribal. And tonight as Spence stood beside Sam at the sink peeling a potato as though his life depended on it, it was one of the best moments of her life.

"It's hard to get just the skin," he said, pushing the peeler against the brown skin and coming away with lots of white potato flesh.

"Well," Sam said, "it takes a gentle touch. It's not like sharpening a pencil." She closed the oven door on the pork roast she'd put in and leaned over to show Spence how it was done.

My first mom lesson, she thought. *Never thought it would be about potatoes.*

"I'll do it." Jennifer swept in, curling her arms around Spence, blocking Sam with her back.

Well. Sam tried not to be disheartened. Or offended that Jennifer saw her as such a threat.

Jennifer had brought him here, after all. She'd opened this door and it sucked that she kept slamming it in Sam's face.

"Sam, I could use your help with these veggies," Deb said, sitting beside Christina making the salad at the table.

"You bet," Sam said, forcing herself to sound unbothered, because she could feel Jennifer's gaze on her back as she walked over to Deb and Christina.

She took over cucumber duties and watched as Jennifer and Spence cut the potatoes and put them on the stove to boil, feeling unbearably left out.

You just found out about him, she reminded herself. *And he's leaving in two days. Let's not get ahead of ourselves.*

She tried to warn herself to not rush into feeling something for this boy. But rushing in emotionally was what she did. It was how she worked. It was why she was here, living above her women's shelter.

It was how she'd been with J.D. It was...depressing.

Not personal, she reminded herself, when her emotions, black and poisonous, bubbled up from her chest.

"Should I set a plate for J.D.?" Deb asked, her brown eyes centered on Sam's face. "He's staying, right? I saw him move his bags up to your room."

All the eyes in the kitchen swept to her and by sheer force of will she kept her skin from going red. "He can take care of himself. Don't worry about it."

"That guy?" Christina asked. "He lives here?"

"No," Sam said.

At the same time Deb said, "Sometimes."

Well, that certainly cleared up the whole situation.

"What's the J.D. stand for?" Jennifer asked, and it took all of Sam's strength to meet those eyes.

"Not Jonathon David," Spence said, before Sam had decided whether or not to lie. He hopped off the stool he'd been standing on.

"How do you know?" Sam asked, her voice sharp.

Spence shrugged. "I asked him."

Everyone turned back to their jobs, the attention blissfully off her, and she was able to put down the knife and clench her shaking hands together.

She wanted to believe J.D. had lied to the boy but her gut —her gut that knew a lie from the truth almost every time— knew that J.D. had lied to her.

About his name.

And that felt unbearably personal.

∼

It was midnight before J.D. went inside the shelter. He used his key to open the back door into the kitchen. Daisy growled at him briefly, then recognized him and trotted over for a head scratch.

J.D. obliged, scrubbing the dog's ears the way she liked.

He'd managed to avoid Sam and the boy. Going into town to talk to the police chief had been a waste of time, but at least it killed a few hours. And, hopefully, alerted the guy to watching out for strangers in town during the next few days. But he doubted it. Try as he might, J.D. did not get along well with others, especially when those others were small-town police chiefs.

Uncle Milo had been a pro working with local police. Within ten minutes Milo could get any man or woman with a badge to promise to call Milo with whatever information he'd been after. And they'd do it, too.

Milo had been like that. A box of pastries, a couple stories about the wife and grandkids he didn't have and people would do just about anything for the guy.

J.D. had not inherited that talent.

Milo was fond of saying that J.D. had more of his father in him than was good for anyone. That he'd said it with such affection was the only reason J.D. hadn't tried to beat an apology from him.

"I'll teach you how to get past it," Milo had said, that morning a million years ago standing in the parking lot outside of Wilhelm Juvenile Detention Facility. "You don't have to be like your dad."

J.D. hadn't believed Milo at the time, having just done eighteen months for assault. But no one else had been waiting for him in that parking lot.

Milo took J.D. in when no one else would. Milo shared

his condo, his life and his livelihood with his sister's boy and never asked for anything in return.

J.D. wondered now, climbing the steps to Sam's apartment, his sleeping bag under his arm, what Uncle Milo would have thought about Sam. And Spencer. And what J.D. was doing about them.

He wouldn't be proud, that's for sure.

He shook his head, hoping to clear his thoughts. Having Uncle Milo in his head made him morose. And remembering juvie and his father made it hard for him to breathe.

The door at the top of the steps creaked slightly and he braced himself for the scent of roses and the haunting ghostlike images of Sam that he saw wherever he looked.

He wasn't prepared to see the real thing.

Sam sat in her rocking chair, the sulfuric smell of anger surrounding her like a cloak.

Light from the moon took shards from the darkness, jagged slices of light that revealed her hands, clenched in fists. Her bare feet. Her eyes filled with loathing.

"What's your name, you bastard," she hissed.

Her anger was a match to his and he had to look away, walk away. Stepping to the couch, he deliberately untied his sleeping bag, unfolding it out over the cushions with a snap.

"What is your name?" she asked again.

He could feel her over his shoulder. He could smell her, touch her if he wanted to. If he wanted to, he could grab her, wrap his fingers in her hair and kiss her until all the anger that crashed up against his control turned to something else. Something thicker and hotter and a hell of a lot safer.

But he was never going to touch Sam again.

"One answer," she said, grabbing on to his shoulder and tugging. He let himself get spun. Her whole body thrummed with emotion like a string pulled too tight and moments away from breaking. "One miserable scrap of truth, J.D., for all the times I slept with you."

The shadows in the room couldn't hide her shame, and something that might have been guilt, might have been regret, flickered over his conscience.

He never wanted her to be ashamed.

"It doesn't matter, Sam." He sighed. "Let it go."

"I can't, J.D.," she said, her voice rich with sarcasm. "Because our son is downstairs. Our son. The boy I made with you. And I put the name Jonathon David on the birth certificate because that is who I thought you were."

He said nothing, wishing he hadn't been thinking of the past, because he felt drained. Where his outrage should have been there was only emptiness. A great big nothing at the center of him.

"Who is the liar, now?" she asked. "Is there any part of you that was real?"

Too much, he almost said, despite how hard he tried to keep things separate.

"I didn't lie to you about my name," he said, remembering that morning in bed years ago. She'd lain against him, her breasts against his chest, her leg thrown across his, the sunlight turning her hair to fire and tried to guess what the letters J.D. stood for. When she guessed Jonathon David, he didn't say no. "I just didn't tell you the truth."

"And you called me a coward," she spat. "Why?" Her eyes suddenly flooded with a misery that he could feel like a punch in the gut. "Why did you have to lie to me?"

He could only stare at her, feeling her pain and his own combined. A sickening mix.

"I never wanted you to be hurt," he said, his voice thick.

She laughed wildly. "That's why you lied? To prevent me from being hurt?"

"You don't know who I am," he whispered, thinking of his work. His father. Juvie. The blood on his hands. The blood in his veins.

"Yeah," she said, grim as stone. "So I've learned."

"I didn't want you to find—" He stopped himself, jabbed his fingers through his hair. All the rules he'd made for himself were being broken, destroyed, his secrets spilling out like brains on his bedroom floor.

"Find you?" she asked, incredulous. "You gave me your cell-phone number. I could find you anytime I wanted."

"Drop it, Sam," he said through clenched teeth.

"No." She shook her head. "I can't. I can't let it go. You're in my house. You're in my head. You're a liar and a coward and I can't forgive myself for the way I felt about you."

Her words echoed around the silent room.

But still he didn't say anything.

Her eyes filled with tears that she quickly blinked away and for some stupid reason he wanted to stroke her face, that smooth silky skin of her cheek, and tell her that it was better this way. That she'd get over it. Move on.

"You're a bastard," she spat. "Whatever your name is."

She walked away, head held high, an outraged queen.

And because he'd never meant to hurt her or make her ashamed of what had been between them and couldn't stand, even considering what she'd done, to hurt her this way now, he opened his mouth and did something stupid.

"Jakos Diavoletes," he said and she stopped and turned, a slice of moonlight across her lips. Her eyes in darkness. "That's my name. And I didn't tell you because I didn't want you to find out about me."

"Find out what?"

"It doesn't matter now, does it?" he asked.

"J.D.?" She shook her head, as if she didn't understand and he turned away, raw and naked.

"You got what you wanted," he said. "Now go to bed."

He kicked off his shoes, pulled his shirt over his head and still she stayed. Still she watched. The air was so hot it might have been on fire. His skin soaked up her gaze and desire pounded through his blood in a sudden rampage. He wanted to push her against the wall, shove himself into her, bury his confusion and hurt into the welcoming center of her body.

And she wanted him; he could feel her craving, her weak-kneed lust from across the room. Hell, he'd be able to feel her across the state.

"Was there something else you wanted?" he asked, his voice a mocking invitation.

She stepped forward, the light falling across her face, her eyes revealed and he was hard in a heartbeat. Her hot gaze raked him from head to foot, destroyed him and he wanted to forget what she'd done and who he was and push her down on the floor.

For a moment it seemed as though she was going to take another step toward him. And if she did, he'd take that as an equal interest in his floor fantasy and screw his promise to never touch her again.

Come on, something dark in him whispered, something that wanted him to lose all control and take these crushing feelings he had out on her gorgeous and willing body. *One more step, baby.*

He lifted his hand, stroked his chest, the flat plane of his stomach. His fingers, numb and thick, pulled the button on his jeans.

"It won't work," she said, her voice a dry gasp.

"It already is," he said, laughing at her. At him. At the

whole damn situation. He was sleeping on the couch, for chrissake, and they wanted each other so bad all it would take was a touch and they'd be in pieces.

She flinched at his laughter and the moment was over, the heat between them turning frosty.

"I never really knew you at all, did I?" she asked, her voice unbearably sad, her eyes decades older.

"It's not your fault," he told her. "You knew what I wanted you to know."

"Which was nothing," she whispered.

It wasn't true. She knew more about him than most people. But the important things, he'd kept hidden.

"Which was nothing," he agreed and she turned, walking through light only to end up back in the darkness.

8
———

Usually Sam loved mornings. She woke with the sunrise, filled with an enthusiasm, a clear-headed, goal-oriented joy in the day. In living. Working.

She'd been told by more than one roommate that all of this was incredibly annoying.

J.D. at one point, his head buried under a pillow, had said that all morning people should be shot. At dawn.

The thought of J.D. galvanized her and she flipped her ladybug sheets off her body, ready, if not willing, to get on with the day.

It was still early yet, so she knew he'd be sleeping. All naked and stretched out on her couch, his skin the color of caramel in the dawn light.

Last night had been dangerous; the coiled tension between them had turned quickly into lust. And she'd been filled with a need to make him pay for his lies with his body.

Stupid. Reckless. A little creepy. But there you have it. Had she not been so terribly saddened by the truth of how little she meant to him, she might have taken him up on that blatant invitation in his eyes.

Find out what about him? she wondered, now remembering his stupid rationale for lying to her about his name. What, exactly, was he so afraid she'd find?

His address, she guessed. He worried she'd show up on his door one day, expecting more from him than he'd ever been willing to give.

Well, despite last night and the moments of lunacy in the moonlight, he had nothing to worry about. There was nothing she wanted from him anymore.

She pulled on a pair of yoga sweats and a short-sleeved T-shirt, scraped her hair into a ponytail and took a deep breath before opening her door, bracing herself for all that skin on her couch.

But her couch was empty.

His sleeping bag was rolled up on the floor.

And J.D. was nowhere to be found.

She shut down the curiosity and decided to count her blessings. She didn't have to see him, and that was reason enough to be happy. She thought about making coffee in her own apartment and decided not to press her luck. If he was in the bathroom, or perhaps out for a run only to return, she'd rather be out of here.

Stepping lightly down the steps not wanting to wake anyone who might still be sleeping, she crept into the kitchen and put on a pot of coffee.

She swung open the door to the common room intending to get the newspapers they had delivered only to be brought up short by the sight of Spence sitting cross-legged on the couch.

Daisy the vicious guard dog flopped over on her back beside him, her pink belly exposed. The couches were forbidden territory for sure and as soon as Daisy saw Sam she jumped down and curled up on the floor at Spence's feet.

"Hi," he said, flipping his notebook closed as if caught doing something he shouldn't.

Spence's red hair was a wild mess on his head, creases from his sheets lined his cheek and his Baltimore Zoo T-shirt was still a size too big for him.

But he was beautiful. So beautiful her heart hurt.

"Hi," she answered, rubbing her sternum. "What-cha doing?"

He shrugged and toyed with the metal coil of his notebook.

"Where's your mom?"

"Sleeping," he said. "She sleeps a lot."

Classic sign of depression, she thought, feeling another surge of sympathy for Jennifer and Spence.

"You hungry?" she asked.

"I had a banana."

"Thirsty?"

He pointed to a glass of milk sitting on a coaster on the table next to him.

She was all out of motherly type questions to ask the boy. He was fed. Watered. She didn't want to go for a walk and wasn't about to ask him if he wanted to.

Good God, Sam, he's not a pet, she chastised herself.

"You, ah..." She looked at his notebook. "Think of more questions you wanted to ask me?"

His lip kicked in a smile and she was stupidly glad to be the reason it was there. "Sort of."

"Well, all right," she said. "Let me get some coffee and I'm all yours."

She turned, intending to come back with her mug, and

was surprised when he followed her, pulling himself up to the kitchen table like he was at home.

"Fire away," she told him.

"Have you always lived here?" he asked and while she knew she shouldn't be stunned by the kid's questions after the oral medical exam from yesterday, the question still seemed to come from left field.

"No," she answered, taking a seat across from him. "I came to work here after I graduated from college in Asheville and I lived in an apartment about thirty minutes away from here just outside of Raleigh."

"I like Asheville. We used to go there for vacations."

"I like it, too," she said.

"Did you go to the concerts in the park?"

"Whenever I could."

They grinned at each other and she could almost see him in that park, one of those kids running wild or dancing on the grass during big band night. Although, she had to amend the vision. Spence, as he was now, didn't look like a wild runner, or a dancer. She hoped, she really did, that before all of this with his father happened he'd been one of those kids, flopped out on blankets under the stars.

"So when did you move here?"

"When the last director retired," she said. "A little over ten years ago."

"Do you like it here?" he asked, tilting his head in that totally J.D. way.

"I love it here," she said honestly. "This is my home."

"Did you grow up in a place like this?" he asked.

She shook her head, catching on to his line of questioning. "Nope," she said. "I grew up in Texas. It was really normal. I had a mom and a dad and a cousin who I played with. But my boyfriend from high school went to school in Asheville, so I followed him out here."

"Is his name Jonathon David?" Spence asked, his eyes big in his little head. Sam shook her head, wishing the question wasn't so sad. Wishing the whole situation wasn't so impossible.

No, she wanted to say. *Your dad is here somewhere. He's just too scared and too stubborn to understand that you need him. That this is important.*

"Sorry, kiddo," she said. "We broke up pretty soon after I moved out here."

Spence chewed on his lip and wrote some things down. Sam had to stop herself from craning her neck to see what he'd written.

The muffled sound of a cell phone ringing brought Spence's head up. "That's my mom's phone," he said, looking toward the hallway like an expectant puppy. But when Jennifer didn't appear, his bright eyes and smile faded.

"Can I ask you a question?" Sam asked, slowly spinning her mug on the table.

He shrugged. "Sure."

"Is your mom okay?"

The kitchen was so silent she could hear Daisy breathing under the table. "She's better than she was," he finally said.

"What was she like before?"

"She didn't get out of bed." His voice was so small in the empty kitchen. And he somehow looked both younger and older than his nine years. She wondered when was the last time he'd had fun.

"What happened to your dad?" she asked, watching him, absorbing him and wishing she could reach out for him.

"He died. He was sick for a long time..." His voice

cracked and Sam thought she might cry. Might just splinter under the weight of the boy's unexpressed grief. "In the hospital and then he died."

"And that's when your mom stopped getting out of bed?"

Spence nodded, his gaze again riveted to his notebook, and she had the impression of a bomb about to go off. He was too still. Too quiet. Too controlled. He was nine, for crying out loud. Then she realized how many hours Spence must have sat in a hospital room. In waiting rooms. Told to be quiet. Be still. Be careful.

He needed time to run around. Be loud. Remember what nine-year-olds were supposed to do.

"Yesterday she laughed," he said. "I thought that was a good thing."

"It is a good thing," she said emphatically, and his gaze darted up and met hers gratefully.

"Yeah," he said. "And she ate dinner last night."

"A lot of it," Sam said, exaggerating slightly.

"And we read to each other before bed. Like we used to."

"Wow." Sam nodded. "Sounds like you're doing all the right things, Spence. You're taking really good care of her."

And bingo.

Spence smiled. His whole face illuminated from the bones to his curls to the sheet crease on his skin, as if joy and relief just poured out of him.

"Do you have any more questions?" she asked, gesturing to his notebook.

He shut the cover and pulled it in closer, shaking his head. "Maybe later."

"Okay." Sam checked her watch. It was Sunday. Nothing much going on on Sundays. J.D. was around somewhere, and so was a mafia princess. But she wasn't going to think about those things right now. "You want to play a game?"

"What kind of game?" Spence asked, watching her from beneath red-gold eyelashes.

"Well, I haven't played UNO in a while and I—"

"UNO's my favorite," Spence said.

"Mine, too," she said, smiling broadly. Life was strange, she thought. So much was wrong in her world. But because this boy was here, with his questions and seriousness, his beautiful eyes and terrible sadness, everything seemed somehow okay. Somehow manageable. Somehow better.

For the first time regret seized her. Had she kept Spence, perhaps her life wouldn't be so focused on work. So lonely.

"I'll go get the cards," she said, jumping up from the table.

JENNIFER WAS SITTING beside Doug's bed. Again. Watching his chest lift and fall. Lift and fall. Knowing there wasn't going to be any hesitation. That, should she allow it, his chest would never stop its measured undulation thanks to the machine he was attached to.

She sat back, weary to the bone just as one of the machines started blaring a terrifying alarm. Jennifer hurled herself across his bed, trying to gauge which machine hooked up to which part of his body was malfunctioning.

Lungs. Heart. Kidneys.

More alarms. More blaring. Her heart pounded in her chest. Which one? Which one?

"Jennifer?"

She whirled to face her husband, ashen and so thin it nearly killed her to look at him. But there were no intubation tubes, no oxygen mask. He was smiling.

"It's your phone, sweetie," he told her. "Not my heart."

Jennifer crashed into consciousness with a sickening impact. Sitting up, the reality of her surroundings, the shelter's rough sheets, beige walls, snapped her out of her dreamland. Nauseous and disoriented, she looked for Spence, panic a flash flood in her bloodstream. But then she saw the note next to her ringing phone. He was reading in the common room. Relieved, she grabbed her phone from the bedside table.

"Yes?" she barked, pushing her hair from her face.

"Jennifer? It's Kerry."

"Waldo?" she asked, reality like an IV drip coming to her slowly, one blessed bead at a time. "What time is it?"

"About eight on Sunday. I've been trying to get you at home."

"I'm not there."

Kerry laughed. "So I gathered. I know you don't like us using this number, but it's an emergency."

Uh-oh. Kerry Waldo, her producer—or maybe former producer, depending on whether or not the station was going to hold all these unpaid leaves against her—was calling her with an emergency.

It was almost like old times.

If old times included spending the night at homeless shelters and dreaming of her dead husband.

"What's up?" She swung her feet to the floor.

"Annabelle Greer wants to do an interview."

Everything went still. Annabelle Greer. Jennifer waited for the rush of excitement, the old thrill that used to fill her at the prospect of such a story. God. Annabelle Greer. It was once in a lifetime. Jennifer's very specific career dream come true.

And Jennifer felt nothing.

"That's great," she said with as much enthusiasm as she could fake. Kerry laughed.

"You're kidding, right?" Kerry asked. "You've been hounding that woman for three years."

That was three years ago. A lifetime and a husband ago.

"I'm on vacation."

Kerry was silent and Jennifer could tell it wasn't one of the good types. Kerry was biting her tongue.

"It's been six months, Jennifer—"

"So I should be over it? My husband died, Kerry."

"I know, I know, Jennifer. I'm not saying you should be over it. I'm saying maybe work would do you some good. Maybe it's time to get out among the living."

"The living?" Jennifer asked. "What the hell is that supposed to mean?"

"It means Doug died, not you," Kerry said. "You've spent most of the past year in a hospital and your bed. And right now the woman you have been wanting to interview your entire career has agreed to sit down with you. Her husband's out of the White House, her son is all over the gossip magazines. She's got a blockbuster on her hands with her latest book and she wants to talk to you. The former First Lady of the United States will only do this interview with you. No you, no interview."

Jennifer's hands shook. Fear like a knife slid right through her guts. Right through her heart. "I'm not—" She swallowed, awash in doubt. "I don't think I can—"

"She felt terrible about not being at Doug's funeral," Kerry said and Jennifer's eyes slid shut. "She didn't want the press to be there. So she's invited you up to her parents' place on the Hudson. I'll produce. Just you, me, Eric on camera and her."

She nearly laughed. *Just me and the former First Lady. Me*

and my idol. My hero. My son's favorite author. My husband's godmother.

But, God, where was her excitement? Where was her hunger, her instincts? Doug took everything with him. Everything that was her was gone. Except for Spence. Without Spence here she'd probably melt into her sheets.

Oh, God, if that wasn't reason enough to get back to work she didn't know what was.

"When?" she asked.

"You'll do it?"

"I'm just asking when, Kerry. Don't get excited."

"Wednesday morning," Kerry answered. "But we'll need you tomorrow."

She sighed. "I'll call you back in a few hours," she said, hung up and then flopped sideways onto the bed.

J.D. APPROACHED the kitchen with his Leatherman tool and a new lock from the hardware store. He was braced for Sam, having been able to smell roses and coffee over the smell of slightly industrial disinfectant that usually filled the shelter.

His whole body went on high alert the second he stepped through the door.

I've got to get out of here, he thought. Tired of his body being a dog on a leash at the mere thought of her. *Come on, Greg*, he thought. *Make the boyfriend talk and set me free.*

J.D. had slept for all of thirty seconds last night, lying on her lumpy fold-out couch, the smell of her a torment in his head, the memories of what they'd done on that couch in the past a stone in his stomach.

He felt full of her, like there was a part of her living

under his skin and he had to be on guard against it at all times.

He pushed open the door to the kitchen.

So, in a sense, he was constantly braced for her.

But he wasn't braced for the kid. Could never be braced for the sight of that boy.

"Skip," Sam said, laying down UNO cards with flourish. "Skip, oh, and look at this, another skip." She grinned at Spence, but then caught sight of J.D., breathless and stupid in the doorway.

It was so like that vision he had. The three of them around a table. Laughing.

But the smile fled from her face and she laid down another card. "Yellow seven," she said and cleared her throat.

Any joy in the room had been sucked out by his arrival and part of him wanted to turn around. Walk right back out. But he had this lock in his hand and there was work to do.

And that's my son.

Damn, thinking like that wasn't going to do him any good. Wasn't going to do anyone any good.

But still he didn't leave.

"You know," Spence said, groaning. "I'm a kid and most adults let kids win."

She's not most adults.

"I'm not most adults," Sam said. Her gaze flickered up to J.D. "Was there something you needed?" she asked, cool as winter, and Spence turned around to see who she was talking to.

The effect of his own eyes in that miniature body hadn't lost any impact. They still seemed like a laser cutting right through his guts and sinew. To the heart of him.

Spence lifted the fingers he had curled around the back of the chair in a small wave and J.D. forced himself to act.

"You need a new lock on the window," he said, striding across the room like it was a battlefield he was taking over. He ignored the boy's little wave and felt like a jackass for doing it. J.D. was treating Spence like he had the plague when he was just a kid trying to be polite. Yet J.D. couldn't stop.

"Oh," Sam said, and he could feel her eyes on the naked skin of his neck. "Thank you."

Her gratitude made him churlish. The whole damn situation made him want to throw things through the window.

"You're welcome," he snapped.

"Grouchy," Sam whispered, no doubt to Spence in an effort to clear the toxic air J.D. had brought in the room.

Spence laughed and they resumed playing cards. J.D. took a deep breath, unaware he'd been holding it.

He could practically see Uncle Milo, shaking his head with disgust.

"Spence is just a kid," Milo would say. "He doesn't deserve this."

J.D. leaned against the counter and began to unscrew the bolts on the old lock.

Uncle Milo would do the right thing. Like the old man had done with him. Just thinking that made guilt swell in his throat like vomit.

If Uncle Milo could claim him, despite what J.D. had done, why couldn't J.D. be decent to this kid?

The phone in Sam's office rang and the sound of her chair scraping across the linoleum seemed loud.

"I'll be right back," she said to Spence, then seemed to wait. No doubt wondering what terrible thing J.D. would do if left alone with the kid.

I'm not a monster, J.D. wanted to snap. *I'm not going to hurt him.*

But then he wondered if she'd searched the Internet about him. And found out that he was indeed a monster.

"He's fine here," J.D. said, tossing the busted lock in the sink and making a point of not looking at Sam. "I'll keep an eye on him."

He felt the moment he was alone in the room with the kid like a cold wind at his back.

"Whatcha doing?" the boy asked.

J.D. glanced quickly over his shoulder, getting an impression of red hair and blue-gray eyes filled with a wary curiosity.

"Putting on new locks." He ripped open the packaging for the new lock, spilling the parts onto the counter in clumsy haste. He swore under his breath.

"I heard that," Spence said.

Great.

"You want to play cards?" Spence asked. "You can have Sam's hand."

"I'm fixing the lock."

"Right." Cards slapped against the table and J.D. heard the kid get up, his bare feet almost silent against the floor. "Can I help?" he asked.

J.D. turned and nearly took the kid's head off with his elbow. "Dad always let me help," the kid insisted. J.D. could not look at the boy's earnest face. "He said I did a good job."

"There's not much—"

"He gave me a tool set for Christmas last year. A real one. Not a kid set."

J.D. could barely breathe. His brain was turning to mush, a pile of goo inside his skull. The boy's chatter was like a spell. He couldn't move.

"Here." Spence braced his arms, so skinny under the wide sleeves of his T-shirt, on the counter and shimmied himself up and beside J.D. in a second.

The silk of Spencer's hair brushed J.D.'s arm and he jerked away as if he'd been brushed by live wires.

"I can hold it," Spence said, blinking at him. "And you do the screws."

J.D. looked at the boy and saw himself. Saw himself at sixteen, alone and scared and wanting, despite all the bravado he'd learned at Wilhelm, to help. To be useful.

He'd wanted more, of course. J.D. had looked up at Uncle Milo and wanted something clean, something to wipe away some of the black swill of his life.

He hoped, again, that Spence would never know that darkness.

"My dad died," Spence said and the screwdriver fell from J.D.'s hands, banging off the sink.

Don't do this to me. Don't make this so hard. I'm trying to do the right thing here.

"I'm sorry," J.D. said, picking up the screwdriver. "About your dad."

"It's all right. I mean it's not. But—" The boy shrugged, digging his thumbnail in the grout around the stainless steel sink.

"I know," J.D. said, because he did know. He knew how things could be so wrong, all the way down deep, but on the surface be okay.

Spencer looked up, his eyes so clear, such a beautiful mix of blue and gray like the ocean off the coast. The boy tilted his head, his eyes touching on every one of J.D.'s features as if he were looking in a mirror.

"Do you want me to help?" Spence asked.

J.D. could barely nod. But a light returned to Spence's

eyes and he maneuvered to sit on the edge of the sink, his bare feet planted on either side of the drain, his knees pressed tight together.

J.D. tried not to breathe. He tried not to feel. Or think. Or want. Or wish. But it was all right there anyway, as real as the smell of bananas coming off his son. And things inside of J.D. broke. Walls he'd erected in juvie, under the brutal hands of his father, walls that were reinforced every day doing his job, all collapsed and he found himself wanting something. For the first time in years.

He wanted to reach out to this kid.

"J.D.?"

"My name is J. D. Kronos," he whispered. "I'm your dad."

9

Sam held herself up by sheer force of will. Her knees were water and her hands, braced on the door frame of her office, felt like cobwebs.

Closing her eyes couldn't block out the scene in her kitchen. It was burned into her head, her heart branded by the look in J.D.'s eyes as he stared down at Spencer.

J.D., at that moment, was so naked, so vulnerable, so real. And it only proved that he'd never been half as vulnerable, half as naked, half as real with her.

She'd never seen that look in his eye, that caution and worry. J.D. looked so young staring down at Spence. His arms at odd angles, his eyes wide.

He looked like a boy.

And she wanted, she wanted so badly—knowing it was stupid and useless and practically suicidal—to stroke his forehead, curl him against her chest, hold him tight warding off those feelings of doubt that she saw in his eyes.

"You said your name wasn't Jonathon David," Spencer said and Sam's head spun. J.D. had claimed Spencer. He'd done it.

"It's not," J.D. said, his voice a gruff whisper in the quiet kitchen. "It's Jakos Diavoletes. Sam thought my name was Jonathon David."

"Jakos Diavo—" The boy stumbled over the foreign name and Sam stepped backward into the shadows of her office. Her heel hit the boxes of shampoo and she lowered herself onto them, feeling older than dirt. Older than the world. Something ugly filled her—a green, greedy monster.

You're better than this, she tried to tell herself. *You know better.*

But it was one more thing about herself that this situation with J.D. had ripped away.

She wasn't above jealousy.

She was envious of her son. Of what J.D. was giving that boy.

What's wrong with me that I would begrudge Spencer this moment?

But even as she thought it, she knew it wasn't true. Not entirely. It's that J.D., not once in ten years together, had ever given her this moment. He'd surprised her, brought her a guard dog, listened to her fears late at night. She'd thought she had part of him, carried something of him with her, in her, around her.

But he'd never given anything of himself. Not the way he was giving to Spencer.

And she felt like she'd given so much of herself. Every time.

"Jakos. The *J* makes a *Y* sound. Diavoletes," J.D. said. "It's Greek."

"I'm Greek?" Spence asked, as if there might be superpowers involved in such a thing.

There was a long pause and finally J.D. cleared his throat and said, "Yes. I guess you are."

J.D. had claimed Spencer.

She knew she shouldn't care. She was still angry, furious with him. With herself. But it still hurt.

Almost more than she could bear.

Sam leaned forward and swung her door shut.

JENNIFER MANAGED to pull herself out of her bed and into the clothes she'd worn yesterday. Everything hung from her body like a sack.

I'm a scarecrow, she thought, catching sight of herself in the cheap mirror above the cheaper chest of drawers. Doug had always called her elegant. Fragile, even. Audrey Hepburnesque. Now, she looked like bones in loose flesh.

She leaned closer to the mirror, pulling taut the newly sagging skin at her jawline. How had she gotten here? A face-lift candidate.

None of that mattered now. She'd packed their bags, leaving out a clean pair of shorts and a T-shirt for Spence. She'd gone so far as to make up their beds, tucking down the sheets just as she'd found them last night.

She looked around the room, and it was as if they'd never been here at all. Which is how she wanted it. She wished she could just reach into Spencer's head, tuck down his memories, making it seem as if he'd never met Sam. Never seen this place.

It was time to go.

Spence had met Sam, asked his questions. Life was calling her back to Baltimore.

The First Lady, after all, was waiting.

She paused, searched hard inside herself for some kind of reaction, but again, there was nothing.

She left the room, stepping into the hallway toward the kitchen. Following the smell of coffee and the sound of her son's voice and, surprisingly, the deeper vibration of an adult male's voice.

She sped up, encouraged by some nameless panic, nearly erupting into the kitchen, only to discover Spence and that man, J.D., putting screws to a lock on the window.

"Hey, Mom!" Spence cried, his face flushed with excitement, his eyes glittering with an inner energy she hadn't seen in eons.

It was blinding and beautiful.

"Guess what, Mom?" Spence asked and she opened her mouth to say what, but apparently he was in no need of prompting. "I'm Greek."

"You're what?"

"Part Greek. This is J.D." Spence gestured to J.D., who nodded at her without making eye contact. Her stomach contracted in sudden apprehension. "He's my dad."

It wasn't the words—a fool could see that this silent man was Spencer's biological father. It wasn't even the way J.D. looked at Spence, as if the boy was a gift-wrapped box he didn't know what to do with.

It was the way Spencer looked at J.D. The worship blooming in his eyes.

Just like that, Doug was gone.

"Can I have a word with you, Spencer?" she said, her voice sharp and biting, but only J.D. seemed to notice, turning to her with a sudden tension.

"Sure, but, Mom, guess—"

"Now!" she snapped and Spencer's mouth fell open.

I'm sorry, she wanted to say. *I don't know what I'm doing.* "Please," she murmured to soften the blow.

Spencer, silent, his inner light extinguished, jumped off the counter.

"I'll see you later," J.D. said to Spencer though his eyes were on Jennifer. She couldn't read them, but they made her uncomfortable. Scared even.

The man couldn't be further from Doug if he'd tried.

I want out of here, her heart screamed. *Right now.*

"What's going on, Mom?" Spencer asked as they walked toward their room. But she knew, as much as she wanted out, Spencer wanted to stay and a battle she barely had the energy for was coming her way.

"Why don't you get dressed," she said, stalling for time. "Then we'll talk."

∼

J.D. WATCHED the boy and his mother leave and had to fight himself to stay put. It wouldn't be cool to follow, to listen at the door. There was no call for surveillance.

But, man, ten minutes with the boy and J.D. hated to see him walk out of the room like that. Cowed. All the sparkle in his eyes gone.

Sam entered the kitchen behind him. Not that she touched him. Or he heard her. It was nothing that concrete. He just knew she was there even though she was feet away.

When would this end? "You told him?" Sam whispered.

He cleared his throat and nodded. "Yeah."

"That must have made him happy," she said. He could hear her trying to smile and it set off a stinging pain in his chest.

"Seemed to," he said and turned back to the lock. He picked up the plastic from the counter and tossed it in the trash, searching for something else to do to keep his hands busy.

"Have you talked to your friend?" Sam asked. "The FBI agent?"

"I left a message this morning," he said, turning slightly to catch sight of her out of the corner of his eye. "He should get back to me soon."

She was pale, her eyes red, and it shouldn't bother him, but it did. She'd been crying. But there was something else about her, something flinty and cold. Something new.

"I'd like this situation with Christina cleared up as soon as possible," she said, her eyes unblinking.

"And why's that?" he asked, though he could sense the answer in the tilt of her chin. It was about time, he thought, even as that stinging pain came back, harder and sharper than before.

"I want you out of my life," she said and turned back to her office.

It was no different than how he felt. No different at all.

So the pain was a bit surprising.

The cell phone in his hip pocket vibrated and he yanked it free. Greg. Finally.

"What?" he barked into the receiver.

"We've got a small problem," Greg said.

"No," Spencer said and crossed his arms. Mom was nuts if she thought he was going to leave now. "No way."

Mom shook her head and pushed the clean clothes at him. "It's not a question, Spence—"

Spence didn't uncross his arms so the clothes fell on the

floor. Mom was mad, and getting madder, but he didn't care. It wasn't fair. She wasn't being fair.

"You just want to leave because you don't want me to have another Mom and Dad."

"Don't be ridiculous," she said, but she was lying. Spence could tell. She'd been lying the whole trip here. For years, every time he brought up meeting his birth mother she'd been trying to change his mind. Well, it wasn't going to work anymore. He'd already met them. And he liked them.

"You didn't want to come here," he yelled. "You never did. You don't like Sam or J.D. and you don't want me to like them either."

"Spence—" Mom reached out for him but he slapped away her hands.

"I'm not a kid, Mom."

"Oh, yes, you are. You're my kid—"

"No, I'm not. I'm Sam and J.D.'s kid."

Mom went white and stumbled backward, falling against her bed. His heart beat so hard his chest hurt.

"I'm sorry," he breathed. "Mom—" He reached out for her and she put up her hand like a crossing guard at a dangerous street. He stopped and chewed on his lip. "I didn't mean that."

"You didn't?" she asked like she didn't believe him.

Spence shook his head. "You're my mom and Dad was my dad. I just—" He stopped because Mom looked like she might cry again and he felt like he was sitting at the bottom of the pool and his lungs were gonna burst if he didn't get some air. "I just like Sam and J.D. and I don't want to go yet."

"I have to go to work, Spencer," she said. Mom cleared her throat and crossed her hands in her lap.

"But you said you weren't going to go back to work until

after summer." If Mom went back to work, he'd be stuck with Mrs. Simms all summer. And Mom going back to work meant she'd work late and on Saturdays and he'd never see her. And then both his parents would be gone.

"I know, but the First Lady has agreed to do an interview."

"But you promised," he said, his voice small and he knew she'd tell him not to whine, that sometimes he couldn't get what he wanted. He knew that. He knew that really well.

But this was important.

"It's just a week," she said, smiling into his eyes with one of her fake smiles that he hated. "Probably only four days. And when I'm done with this we can go on a real vacation. Wouldn't that be fun? Maybe go back to Asheville. You liked it there and—"

"This is a real vacation," he insisted. "This is better than a vacation."

She smiled. "Well, I'm glad you think so but—"

Suddenly the solution dawned on him. "You go to work," he said, grabbing his mom's hand. "And I'll stay here."

"What?"

"It's only four days. You said so yourself. I can stay here and you—"

She shook her head.

"But, Mom—"

"No but Mom." She pulled her hands free and bent to pick up his clean clothes. She held them out to him, her face like a rock. "Come on, get dressed."

"You're not being fair."

"And you're not thinking, Spence. You can't stay here for four days. This isn't just Sam's home, it's her business. Maybe there's no room for you here."

"But we could ask."

"No. We can't."

"Dad would do it," he whispered. Her face got so tight and terrible that he had to look away.

"Dad's not here," she said, her voice like a scream.

"But if he was, he'd say yes." He looked at her and it was really scary because she was so mad and her hands were fists and her eyes were red. "You know he would."

Mom was shaking. Her head, her hands, the ends of her hair.

Dad was the one who had always thought Spence should meet his birth parents. He talked about it a lot, and once he got sick it was about all he talked about. "It's just more love," is what Dad always said to Spencer when, at first, he didn't want to do it. And Dad used to say it to Mom, at night, when Spencer could hear them down in the kitchen arguing about it. "It's just more love, Jen. And when I'm gone, he'll need that. You both will."

They'd really fight then, but Spencer had understood what Dad meant. And so had Mom.

"It's just more love, Mom," he whispered.

"Don't—" she cried and he flinched away from her. "Oh, no," she whispered. "Oh, dear God, what am I doing?" Mom reached for his hand, reeling him in like a fish until he was pressed tight to her chest, her arms around his waist. Under his ear he heard her heartbeat. She kissed his forehead and he felt like crying.

"I'm sorry," she breathed.

"It's okay," he told her quickly.

"No, it's not. It's not okay to yell at you or make you scared."

"I'm not scared," he lied. Her laugh ruffled his hair.

She pulled back and smiled at him, so sad it felt like she was crying. "You're never scared, are you?" she asked.

"I'm scared you're going to say no," he said. "About staying here."

She didn't say anything and he started to think that Dad had gotten it wrong. That Spence had gotten it all wrong.

"I'll have to ask Sam," she said. "So it's still not a yes."

"But it's not a no yet, either," he said, hope a balloon in his chest.

"It's not a no," she agreed, putting her lips right by his ear. She swayed a little and he closed his eyes.

"You're so much like him, you know," she whispered.

Little bombs of relief and love and sadness went off in his chest and he felt like missing his dad was something so big, and so painful he would die from it if he was alone.

And he guessed Mom felt the same way.

He wrapped his arms around her, feeling the bones of her back and pressed his nose in tight to her throat. He took a big breath of his mom's smell, so happy. So glad.

SAM LOOKED up at the knock on her door, both hoping and dreading it would be J.D. standing there, but it wasn't.

It was Jennifer. And she didn't look happy.

"Come on in," Sam said, sitting back from her desk and the doctor's appointments she'd been scheduling for Christina Conti.

"I don't mean to interrupt." Jennifer was back in Ice Queen mode, totally controlled. Totally unemotional.

What an act, Sam thought, looking into the woman's eyes. She didn't know what Jennifer struggled so hard to control but Sam would bet it wasn't pretty.

Jennifer reminded her slightly of J.D., and all of his restraint.

"No worries. Please come in." Sam waved her hand toward the other free chair. "How was your room last night?"

"Fine." Jennifer sat. "Everything is just fine."

Liar, liar. "What can I do for you?"

Jennifer took a deep breath and seemed to hold it while studying her fingernails. "I, ah..." She sighed, then smiled, but her lips trembled. Sam had the very real sense that inside that woman's head barriers were being stormed.

"It's okay, Jennifer," she said. "How can I help you?"

Jennifer's laugh was more like a gasp of pain and she stared up at the ceiling, blinking rapidly. "I want to hate you," she said and Sam sat back, slightly stunned. "I want that J.D. man to get the hell out of here so my son won't want to spend time with him." Tears spilled down Jennifer's cheeks. "I want you to be a terrible person so my son won't like you." Jennifer tipped her head down and looked at Sam with eyes filled with pain. "Can you do that?"

Sam shook her head.

"I didn't think so." Jennifer hauled in a deep breath and pressed away the tears with the palms of her hands.

"Jennifer, I am no threat to you as a mother," Sam said. "I would love to get to know Spence, but I will never be able to take your place. And J.D.—" She stopped, unsure of what she could say about J.D. that would reassure Jennifer. J.D. will only break Spence's heart? Probably not what Jennifer wanted to hear.

"I know," Jennifer said. "In my head I know all this. But in my heart—" Her face twisted with pain. "Sometimes I forget. Actually, most of the time I forget."

"Tell me what I can do," Sam said, charging in the way

she always did, ready to bear the load and ease the pain. "If you two want to stay here longer, or leave right now. Not that I want you to. The shelter is practically empty and I'm really enjoying having—"

"Good, because Spence wants to stay."

"Wonderful, you can stay as—"

"Just Spence," Jennifer said. "I have to go back to work."

Sam blinked at Jennifer, her heart in her throat. "For how long?" Forever? Was that how this would play out? The son she'd given up returned to her?

"Four days," Jennifer said with a slight twist to her lips. "But if it's an inconvenience in any way, he can come with me. He knows that you run a business here and he can't just impose on you."

"It's not an imposition at all. He's welcome to stay. You both are."

Jennifer stared at her, the ice melting, the human woman emerging. "You're a good person, aren't you?"

"I try to be."

"I'm sorry I've been so mean—"

Samantha held up her hand. "Please, no apologies. You've been under a lot of stress lately. Spencer told me about his father."

"It hasn't been easy," Jennifer breathed and Sam felt a pull toward the woman, a kinship that she'd never expected.

Jennifer was doing the best she could and Sam had to admire that. Had to really respect it.

"J.D.?" Jennifer said, watching Sam carefully. "Where is he?"

"He's not out in the kitchen?" she asked, stunned. She'd just told him she wanted him out of her life ten minutes ago. He wouldn't have already acted on that statement, would he?

"Has he left?" Jennifer asked. "Just like that?"

"No." Sam shook her head. He wouldn't do that, not with Christina and the mafia question unanswered. "I'm sure he'll be right back." She tried to put as good a face on it as she could, but she could tell Jennifer wasn't entirely believing or reassured.

"He really is Spencer's father?"

"He is."

"He didn't seem terribly interested," Jennifer said. "And now that he's told Spencer he's got all his hopes up."

"I know." Sam could not believe she was about to defend the man. "But he didn't know about Spence. You've got to give him some time."

Jennifer's eyebrows nearly hit her hairline. "That's quite a secret to keep."

"He's kept a few of his own," she said, not about to explain their relationship.

"Are you two..." Jennifer trailed off.

"Is it any of your business?" Sam asked.

"It is if Spence is going to stay here. If J.D.'s going to just walk away, or..."

It was Sam's fear, too, that J.D.—this new J.D. she didn't know and couldn't depend on—would hurt Spencer with his callousness. Like he'd hurt her.

"I'll take care of J.D.," she said.

Astonishingly, Jennifer smiled. At least Sam thought that slight tip to her lips was a smile.

"Have you been together long?" Jennifer asked.

"Ah." Sam stalled. How was she supposed to answer that? "Yes and no," she finally said. "It's complicated."

"I was with Doug for fifteen years and in some ways, it never got less complicated," Jennifer said. "In some ways it was like we'd known each other our whole lives. And then I could turn around and wonder who this stranger was that I married."

"I know that feeling." Sam laughed without much humor.

"It's worse now with Spence. When I look at him I expect to see my baby and instead there's this little man standing there."

"You should be very proud of him," Sam said.

"I am." Jennifer flushed. "I'm not sure he could say the same right now."

"Don't judge yourself too harshly," Sam said but Jennifer shook her head, apparently not ready to say anything else on the subject.

"At the risk of repeating myself, I'm so glad you're here," Sam said, reaching out and covering Jennifer's cold hand with her own. "Both of you. And I mean it. You can stay as long as you need to."

Jennifer's smile was fragile but real. "Thank you," she said, flipping her hand around and giving Sam's the smallest squeeze, before pulling away.

It wasn't much, Sam thought, but it was the beginning.

"Spence is so excited about staying," Jennifer said and suddenly Sam felt her stomach bottom out.

Spence—her son—was staying. For four days. By himself.

What in the world was she going to do?

10

J.D. wished he could leave. Staring at Serenity House lit up in a bubble of security lights against the black night, he wanted to start the car and drive north, away from what he'd done here today. Away from Sam. Away from Spence.

But because of this mess with Greg, J.D. was firmly locked in here. Christina's boyfriend didn't meet with the bureau last night and was now considered to be on the run.

All day dealing with the fallout and J.D. still couldn't believe it. Greg had lost a seventeen-year-old boy and, with the resources of the government behind him, he still couldn't find the kid.

And so Greg had called J.D., told him to keep a lookout, that the boyfriend was probably headed toward Christina. Greg and his fellow agents suspected the two would try to disappear.

So he was here. Staring at Serenity, at the light on in Sam's room, and he felt as though he'd always been here. That, no matter where he went, part of him would always be here.

Sitting in his car outside Sam's house.

"Get a grip." He swore, then forced himself into action, climbing out of the car and slamming the door behind him.

He'd remained outside most of the day. He'd kept an eye on everyone from his car while he made phone calls. He'd done what he was good at, observed from a distance. Not involved. Not attached.

He'd watched while Jennifer drove away, Spence and Sam standing on the front lawn waving goodbye, and he'd wondered what was going on. Then he'd quickly reminded himself that it didn't change anything. He was working a case and the case remained the same no matter who was here.

At one point, he emailed pictures of Brett Trachten, Christina's boyfriend, to some of his associates in the area, asking them to keep an eye open for the kid.

All in all, he wasn't worried. Frank Conti hadn't moved and he was the big shark to watch.

No doubt, by the morning this thing with the boyfriend would have blown over. Brett Trachten would be caught. Greg would come for Christina and they'd all be sprung from this trap.

The moon was big, bright and so far away—a million miles. The same moon he'd watched from his bedroom window as a kid. The same moon he'd watched through bars at Wilhelm.

He unlocked the front door and slid soundlessly into the dark living room. From her spot by the window Daisy lifted her head and growled, low in her throat.

"Hiya, girl," he murmured and she stood, gave her big body a shake, then came over to lick his hand.

It took J.D. a moment to see Sam sitting at the kitchen table, watching him.

Waiting for him.

"Hi," J.D. said, feeling his chest grow cold under her icy gaze.

"Hello." She managed to be cordial but J.D. heard the emotion under the veneer of politeness. She wanted to kick his ass. The anger that simmered in his blood leaped in response.

"Where have you been?" She took a sip from the mug in her hands, as if it were just a casual question.

He leaned against the door frame, ready to give her the fight she seemed prepped for. "Well, Sam, I didn't think you cared."

"Spencer asked about you all day," she said and part of his self-righteous anger popped and he sagged slightly against the wall. "You told him you were his father and then you left."

"There were some things I had to take care of." Even as the words came out of his mouth he was painfully aware of how lame they sounded. "Important things."

"Really?" she asked, sarcasm like razor wire from her mouth. "More important than Spence?"

There was nothing he could say. He had no defense. He'd hid most of the day because he was scared. The phone call from Greg was an excuse. A weak one. Because the boyfriend wasn't a real threat.

What was real was the regret that he'd told Spencer anything. That he'd stayed in that kitchen this morning when he knew he should have left. Now the boy would want something from him he didn't have to give. That he'd never had to give.

The same things Sam wanted and he'd never been able to give her.

"Why did you tell him? If you feel this way?"

"I don't think that's any of your business, Sam."

"Not my business?" she cried. "I spent the whole day cleaning up your mess, J.D. The kid was heartbroken wondering why you'd leave like that."

Walk away, he urged himself. *Don't get into this fight. You can't win it.* But the caution was useless. He was riveted to the floor, drilled by the look in her eye. Stupidly, foolishly, he tried to redeem himself.

"My buddy with the FBI called," he said and Sam sucked in a deep breath, her anger turning suddenly to a fear so profound he could feel it. "The boyfriend didn't go in last night. He's on the run."

"What does this mean?" she whispered.

"They think he's on the way here."

"Here?" Sam asked. "What are we supposed to do?"

"We wait."

"For?"

J.D. shrugged. "The boyfriend to join the party, I guess."

"Are you being cavalier in an effort to comfort me or piss me off?"

He forced himself not to smile. "Comfort you," he said. "The FBI is looking for him. I've got some guys looking for him. I'm here. Nothing can happen. Besides, he's not the one we need to be scared of. According to Greg, Christina and the boyfriend are very close. He loves her. He won't hurt her."

"Should we send Spence away?" she asked. "He's supposed to stay here for four days while Jennifer gets back to her job." He could tell she was beginning to spin. "We can tell Deb to stay away for a few days. We could call Jennifer and send—"

He touched her arm. A shocking spark of electricity

blew up between them and she shut her mouth so hard her teeth clicked. He pulled away, clenching his hands.

"No," he said. *Why couldn't anything be easy*, he wondered. *Just one damn thing.* He simply wanted to do his job and leave. "I don't think we need to send him away."

"J.D.," she whispered, "what is going on?"

"Nothing we can't handle," he told her. "No one is going to hurt anyone. He's just a kid and he's looking for his girlfriend. It's not a big deal."

She wrapped her arms around her waist and watched him with liquid eyes.

"Sam, I'm serious. It's not—"

"I trust you," she said and the air emptied from his lungs. "I can't believe it. I want to beat some sense into myself, but after everything you've done to me I still trust you. There's something wrong with me. There's been something wrong with me since the moment I met you."

It was a slap across the face, a punch in the gut. Not even her admission of trust could take away the sting. She trusted him, but she didn't want to.

He caught sight of his sleeping bag by the table. "I guess I've been moved," he said and stepped around Sam to retrieve it. To get away from her.

"Spencer is on the couch upstairs. You can have room two. The door is open."

This was for the best, he thought. Being up in that apartment with her was like ripping off his skin.

"Why did you tell him?" she asked again.

He paused in the doorway, knowing exactly what she was talking about. The question had run him in circles all day. And he didn't have an answer so he didn't give her one.

"Yesterday you wanted nothing to do with him," she persisted, despite his silence. "And now you've told him. So why—" She cut herself off. "Forget it," she said, disgust so ripe in her voice the room smelled of it. "I'm so sick of pulling answers from you. You'll either tell me or you won't."

He couldn't say anything and she threw her hands in the air. "Have it your way, J.D. If your life is so damn better all by yourself, be my guest."

He didn't know what she wanted from him. Did she need to hear that he had no freaking clue how to handle this situation? Wasn't that pathetically obvious? Couldn't she see that he was an emotional idiot? Why did she need it spelled out?

She practically threw her coffee mug into the dishwasher, slamming the door so hard the kitchen windows rattled.

"What do you want from me?" he asked as she stomped across the kitchen. Screw trying to guess. Screw always being wrong. He didn't know what the hell he was doing, or supposed to do. If she had an expectation, she could damn well share it.

"I don't want anything from you, J.D.," she said, her chin up, her chest out, her gaze nowhere near his.

He laughed, he couldn't help it. The woman was a terrible liar. Despite the anger, despite the lies, she wanted him so much he could practically taste it. It was there, it was always there. Under her pride, her anger and confusion was her desire for him. Her want and need for him that lived in her like an eternal spring.

And he knew it was there because his want and desire and need for her lived in him, too. A multiheaded monster he couldn't control. And right now, with so much between them, the monster wanted free rein.

"That's not true and you know it," he told her, happy to rock her off that high horse she was perched on. She wasn't perfect. She hadn't handled things right, either. And even though she thought something was wrong with her, given the chance she'd let him right back into her bed.

"It was only sex, J.D.," she sneered, throwing his words in his face. "Remember?"

It had been so much more to him, his time with Sam. It had been a glimpse of something clean. Good. It had been a sanctuary, untouchable, utterly removed from his life.

And her throwing around those words pretending she didn't care pissed him off. The same it had pissed her off when he'd done.

"I'm not talking about sex, Sam. You wanted something from me every single time I walked in the door."

"No," she breathed. "I never expected more—"

"Cut the crap." He leaned across the table toward her, ready to pull out the big guns and reduce her to his same mess. "You wanted me to be your white knight. You wanted me to save you from the way you've been throwing your life into this shelter. You wanted me to be a reason to—"

"Stop it, J.D."

"You wanted to love me." He kept digging at this sore spot he'd known about since the first moment he met her. "And you wanted me to love you."

She breathed hard through her nose and he wondered if she was going to slap him. God, he wished she would. Just so it would give him a reason to put his hands on her again.

"You might be right," she finally whispered. "But if I felt something for anyone, it was the man I thought you were. I don't care about you, Jakos. But you owe Spence something. An apology. Something. He's just a kid, J.D. He doesn't understand." Her righteousness and integrity were a magnet that refused to let go of him. So he stood there feeling the pulse of her anger join his, beating hard in his gut. "I don't under-stand what's wrong in that head of yours, but listen. If you are going to treat Spence this way—letting him in and shutting him out the next minute—then leave right now. Just walk out. I can handle Christina and her father. But I can't handle you hurting that boy anymore because you're such a mess."

She was right. She was more than right. Those words were the same ones that had been running on an endless loop in his head. And once again he didn't have an answer. She acted as if it was so easy to let that kid in.

But that was because, for her, it was.

Not that she'd know, not that he'd ever given her a chance to know, but for him, letting that kid hang around was like dragging his father out of the grave.

Every fear he'd had of turning into the old man was back, haunting him, making him crazy.

I want her to know.

The thought was a quick-acting poison ceasing all lung function.

More times than he could count over the past ten years he had lain in bed with her, watching her sleep, and he'd been so close to telling her. Seconds away from waking her up and spilling all of it, so he could finally be free. Could finally have her or lose her one way or another. Without the lies and secrets.

"I'm scared," he said and they both jerked as if a gun had gone off. He stood at the edge of a cliff, balanced on nothing, a vast, terrible, scary emptiness all around him.

"Of what?" she asked. "Spencer? J.D., he's just a kid, he doesn't want anything—"

"I'm not scared of Spencer." Adrenaline screamed through his system, every instinct demanding he leave. Demanding he keep his stupid mouth shut.

"Then what?" she asked, kindness a thin thread through her voice.

Ah, God, this was the woman he cared for. Caring and compassionate, strong and resilient.

She was a bright light against the blackness that sucked at him.

And that's why he'd never told her. He'd never wanted that blackness to get near her.

"J.D.?"

"I'm scared he'll be like me," he said. The words escaped from his gut, making him light-headed. The world seemed to stop. Sam didn't seem to be breathing. He sure as hell wasn't. "I'm scared he'll be like me, like my father—"

"Your father?" she asked, her voice trembling. He wanted to touch her. He wanted to be held by her and become everything she used to believe he was. The white knight crap. All of it.

But it was never going to happen. He was nobody's white knight. He was a killer, born of killers.

J.D. looked at her face and couldn't believe he'd ever touched her, that she'd let him.

All around him things were breaking. Lines that he'd told himself he'd never cross were being washed away and without them, he didn't know where he was. Who he was.

"We're not—" he took a deep breath "—good men."

"J.D., you're beginning to freak me out."

"I didn't tell you my name because you can find me on the Internet. One Google search and you'll know all about Jakos Diavoletes Kronos and then—" What the hell was he doing? He couldn't go back from this.

"What?" She was somehow closer than she'd been just a second ago. "What would I find out?"

"My dad was a thug. A gun for hire. Mostly for the mob."

"The mob?" There was a buried question in that question and he shook his head.

"Not for Francis Conti, though Frank would know my dad. He'd know me."

"How?"

"Do the search," he said. "I was all over the East Coast papers twenty years ago."

"Why don't you just tell me?" she said, her voice so measured and calm, he felt some of the panic gripping him ease. "Instead of playing whatever game it is you're playing."

Oh, God, if this were only a game. But he was here. Finally. After ten years of circling this spot he was right at his crossroads. He looked at her face and found the strength to put it all on the table.

"My dad drank. A lot. And he wasn't a happy drunk. My mom left when I was nine, she took my sister and probably a couple of broken ribs one night. So then it was just Dad and me and the booze."

"Oh, no." Her voice trembled and he knew she'd seen enough to know what his childhood had been like.

"I don't want your pity." He bit the words out. "I'm telling you so you can finally stop expecting more from me. So you can finally understand that having that kid around me is a bad idea."

"You're not like your father," Sam said, getting right to the point. "You're worried that Spence will be like you and your father and he can't be because you're not like your father."

"You don't know that." It wasn't a denial. It was simple truth. She had no clue, because he'd lied to her from day one. He was exactly like his father and if it hadn't been for Uncle Milo, he'd probably be in jail right along with him.

"I do," she said. "You can give me the wrong name and lie to me, but you can't hide who you are. Not at the core—"

"Sam, when I was fifteen, I beat my dad's head in with a baseball bat."

She gasped, swallowed air as though she was drowning and raised a trembling hand to her mouth.

His entire body buzzed with adrenaline and the urge to run was like a freight train down his spine. But he forced himself to stand his ground, to keep looking right into her eyes. To see the horror.

"You were just a kid," she breathed.

"Hardly." He laughed. He'd stopped being a kid the night his mom left him behind. "I was a man, Sam. Had been for a number of years."

"It was self-defense, wasn't it?" she asked, clearly reaching for straws. "I mean, he was drunk, right? Abusive?"

"That would make you more comfortable, wouldn't it? It would make the way you still feel about me tolerable. Make it okay for me to be around that boy upstairs."

She nodded, her lips bloodless in the moonlight.

Taking a chance, he reached out and touched her, stroked her arm, held her cold hand for the very last time.

"He was drunk. He was abusive," he said.

She sighed with relief and he dropped her hand.

Bye, Sam.

"But it wasn't self-defense. It was premeditated and it would have been murder if the damn bat hadn't slipped out of my hands."

"No." She groaned, her throat working, and he could taste the bile burning in his own throat.

Her breath came in ragged gasps and she backed away, bumping into a chair, putting distance between herself and him.

This was right. The way it should be. A woman like Sam, always looking out for people, should back away from him with horror in her eyes. He should disgust her. Terrify her.

He was, after all, his father's son.

"Three months after putting my dad in the hospital, I was arrested for aggravated assault. I was collecting money for Francis Conti."

Sam reeled backward, her face white with shock. "You worked for Conti?"

"My first job," he said. "Luckily, I got arrested or I'd probably still be working for the man.

"So," he said, his voice mocking. The longer she didn't look at him, the more he hated himself. "You can see my reluctance to welcome the boy into the family. The legacy should have ended with me."

She opened her mouth as if to say something, but no words came out. Tears welled up in those eyes and fell down her cheeks, but still she said nothing. Her lips trembled, her throat bobbed and any moment he expected her to point at the door and tell him to go.

But she didn't.

"J.D., you were a kid. A boy defending himself against his father. The courts—"

"Sam!" he nearly yelled. "I kept a bat under my bed for three months. I waited for him to come after me. I planned it. And then I beat a man up for money, Sam. A man I didn't know. A man who'd done nothing to me. I stepped right into my father's shoes. That's what I am."

She shook her head, blinking rapidly as if she didn't understand. "That's not true, J.D." She reached for him and he slapped her hands away, appalled.

J.D. panted through the pain. He felt sliced in half, like

his guts were outside his body, flinching and cringing from exposure.

But now, at least, he was free. He could stop torturing himself with the fairy tale of life with Sam. Or Spence. J.D., the man he'd been at Serenity, was burned to ash.

He was never going to be anyone other than who he was. The only thing that had changed was that now Sam knew it, too, even though she seemed bent on pretending.

"What is wrong with you?" he said. "You should be kicking me out. You should be protecting that boy from me."

"You were a kid," she said, stepping toward him. "Someone should have been protecting you. What happened when you got out of jail?"

"My uncle Milo picked me up, gave me a job working for him."

"Doing what?"

"He was a private investigator."

"Where's your father?"

"He died ten years ago. In jail. He was stabbed in the gut."

He could tell by her face that none of this was sinking in. She wasn't listening; she was choosing to believe in her fairy tale.

"J.D." Her smile was tremulous. "Don't you see—"

God, she was forgiving. It was ridiculous, really. Sad.

"Are you so desperate," he whispered, deliberately cruel, trying to push her away with both hands, "for someone to love?"

∼

IT HURT, even though she saw right through him and recognized his insult as a desperate attempt to drive her away, it hurt that he so badly wanted to wound her.

But she ached for him. She had wanted to see him vulnerable, to see him honest, but she never expected this pain lived inside of him.

"You don't mean that," she said, shaking her head. Standing resolute. Hoping he'd see that she was on his side. Praying that he wouldn't say something more, something that couldn't be forgiven, or taken back.

He was silent, giving himself away by breaking any contact for just a moment, as though he couldn't stand to meet her gaze. "Do you want me to leave?" he asked, his voice burning through the darkness.

"Leave?" she asked, stunned. "No. Why—"

"Then good night," he said, turning.

"J.D.," she cried. "You can't just walk—"

"I can, Sam. And you should, too. It's late."

And then he was gone.

Sam stood stunned in the kitchen long after he left. Part of her knew she should go after him, prove to him that he wasn't the man he thought he was. That he'd been a boy raised by wolves and he couldn't hold those sins against himself anymore.

But her legs didn't work. Her body was tired. Her soul weary.

The hallway to the bedrooms was too long, miles and miles too long. J.D. was too far away right now. Everything she said would fall on deaf ears. She could scream herself hoarse.

And right now, this night, nothing would get through to him.

Suddenly, everything was too much. Too heavy. Every

facet of her life demanded more of her than she could give. The shelter. The boy. J.D.

Everyone was injured and hurt and bleeding from terrible places and she couldn't keep it all together anymore.

Christ, he beat his father's head in with a baseball bat.

And convincing him that that crime didn't prove his worth was too big a task. A mountain too high.

She didn't have the energy to stand. To walk down that hallway and do battle with his demons.

Tomorrow, she thought. *Tomorrow I will help J.D.*

Tomorrow I will deal with this.

On numb legs she crept up the stairs to her apartment, past Spencer's bed to her bathroom, praying she didn't wake him. Because she really didn't know how to explain to him that she was freaking out because his father had just confessed to murder. Well, attempted murder.

Thank God that bat had slipped.

A hysterical chuckle bubbled out of her throat.

In the darkness she collapsed on the edge of her tub like an old rag.

"Oh, wow," she breathed. Of all the reasons she'd dreamed up for J.D. to lie to her about his identity, she'd never dreamed this nightmare.

Could never dream this nightmare.

Almost made her wish he'd been married or something.

She groaned, rolling her head back on her neck.

Are you so desperate? His words reached up and poked at her tender vulnerable places, just as he'd known they would. What was ridiculous was how she thought she'd kept those secret wishes and dreams hidden for ten years. Her embarrassment burned that he saw so completely through her.

She leaned forward, bracing her elbows on the ceramic

sink, her head in her hands. Her whole body began to shake as adrenaline drained. As her nerves faltered and weakened.

Those angry words he'd thrown in her face tonight were bang on. She'd wanted him to be her white knight. To save her from herself. From a long lonely life living above a women's shelter. She'd wanted him to love her.

And now she wasn't sure what she wanted. Or felt.

She wasn't scared. That she was sure of. If he had wanted to hurt her he would have done it years ago.

And that look on his face when he'd told her...that resigned despair...thinking about it broke her heart. He'd expected her rejection. He'd expected to be kicked out.

It was the same look she saw in the eyes of some of the women who walked in her doors. Women who'd done what they had to survive and society would never understand it. Never forgive it. Women who sold drugs or their bodies to feed their kids were thrown out of a lot of places.

No doubt J.D. had, too.

Sympathy slammed through her and a whole new understanding of him, like a hidden room, appeared. No wonder he didn't tell her the truth. No wonder he reacted the way he had to Spencer. No wonder he was never able to give her more than a few nights a year.

J.D. thought he was a monster.

It was late but she needed some comfort, so she reached over and wrenched open the hot-water valve to her tub. The scent of roses hit her from the bubble bath residue on the enamel and she was assailed by the memory of him in this tub not two days ago.

Her stomach twisted, her heart burned.

He'd been so tender. So caring. In ten years he'd never hurt her. She'd thought over and over again, every time she was with him, that he was the most conscientious man she'd ever met, much less had the pleasure to love.

Try as she might she could not place the crime J.D. had told her about on the man that had sat in that tub with a splotch of suds on his chin.

It just didn't fit.

She shed her clothes like skin and slid into a bath so hot it stung.

She'd wanted vulnerability from the man. Honesty. And she'd gotten it tonight in spades. In horrifying bloody spades. The look on his face when he'd told her he was scared was the worst thing she'd ever seen. He'd been a boy at that moment, all the adult in him stripped away and he was just a scared boy.

Immersed in hot water she still felt a chill down her back, through her bones.

In what J.D. had not said she got a fairly good impression of what his childhood must have been like. Those scars on his body, the old ones he didn't talk about. The ones he'd told her, over and over again, that he didn't remember how they'd come about, she wondered if they'd come from his father.

It explained why he'd do what he did.

She imagined whatever documented abuse his father had dished out over the years had been used as extenuating circumstances, but she didn't know the details.

She thought of that Google search. The answers were out there.

Glancing over her shoulder at the darkness of her apartment, she listened to the laptop downstairs practically whispering her name.

It would be so easy.

Come on, she told herself when her instincts balked, *don't you deserve some answers? Don't you feel entitled to the truth?*

She did. She ached for the truth.

But she couldn't get it from a computer. She'd wanted trust from him. She'd wanted him to give her a piece of himself and tonight he had. Too late for there to be any relationship between them, but she could honor and respect that trust.

J.D. would tell her or she wouldn't know.

She leaned back in the tub and placed a warm washcloth over her eyes. That sympathy she wished she didn't feel morphed and grew and filled her. Not unlike the excitement she used to relish when she knew she'd see him. The warmth, the thrill of his touch. The comfort of his arms, the sound of his breathing in her ear. And she realized she had the only truth she really needed: J.D. was not the monster he thought he was.

11

Spence sat at the kitchen table eating his third piece of cinnamon sugar toast. It was like a doughnut but with butter. No wonder he'd never had this before. Doughnuts were a rare treat and breakfast with Mom usually consisted of yogurt and cereal—nice, but no butter. No heaps of white sugar and no cinnamon.

His mom would totally lose it right now if she saw him. Doughnuts two days ago and now this.

But Sam had said she only knew how to cook three things for breakfast: coffee, ham and egg sandwiches and cinnamon sugar toast.

It would have been rude not to accept her offer to make him breakfast.

But then the phone had rung and she'd plopped the toast, butter, cinnamon and sugar on the table in front of him and ran for her office.

He'd figured out the rest.

But that was a half hour ago and he was beginning to wonder if she was ever going to come back. He was beginning to wonder if staying here had been a mistake.

I miss my mom, he thought.

"Hey."

Spence nearly choked on his toast.

"Hey, Jane," he said, trying to act cool as the pretty pregnant teenager strolled into the kitchen. Her stomach looked bigger than it had the other day, or maybe it was just her T-shirt under the open hoodie she wore was tighter. She looked better, the brown stuff was off her arms and her eyes were sparkly. "How are you?"

"I'm starving," she said.

Excellent. He was a man with breakfast skills. "Can I make you some cinnamon sugar toast?" he asked, expecting her to light up at the offer. It was, after all, sugar for breakfast. But instead she looked, if it was possible, a little whiter. A little sadder.

She pulled the bright pink hoodie she wore higher on her neck and zipped it up past her big stomach.

"Or not," he said, shrugging. "I think there's yogurt and stuff in the fridge."

Spence thought Jane was going to leave, or puke or something. He heard pregnant women acted weird. But after a second Jane smiled and sat down at the table. "I'd love a piece of toast," she said. "With lots of cinnamon and sugar. My mom always made that for me when I was home sick."

"Coming right up," he said, so relieved she wasn't going to upchuck everywhere. He put two slices in the toaster and pushed down the lever. Out of the corner of his eye he watched her pull her cell phone out of her pocket and check something.

"So your mom left," Jane said, putting the phone back in the front pocket of her sweatshirt. "You sad?"

"No," he said fast, because he was a little. "I'm getting to know Sam and J.D. They're, like, my birth parents, you know?"

Her eyes went really wide and she leaned forward. "You're adopted?"

He nodded, focusing on the toast because he felt embarrassed for saying anything.

"Did you always know that?" she asked. "I mean, like, did your mom tell you right away?"

He nodded again.

"Are you pissed?"

"About what?"

"At Sam?" she asked. Her eyes were like lasers or something. "For giving you up?"

The toast popped and he concentrated on spreading an enormous amount of butter on the white bread. "No," he said. "Well, not really. I mean—" He paused to sprinkle his cinnamon sugar mixture on the bread, making sure it got into every corner, and tried to think of ways to put what he'd only written in his notebook into words he could say. "I wonder why she did it."

"She probably didn't know what to do with a baby," Jane said. "She was probably scared."

"Then why'd she get pregnant in the first place if she didn't want a baby?"

"Well," Jane snapped, "sometimes that just happens."

"Oh, man," he said fast, because he was a total idiot. "I'm sorry."

"It's okay," she sighed, brushing her bangs off her forehead. "I mean, I understand why you'd be mad at Sam. But it's not like I was stupid or anything. We used a condom. This was just a total accident." She patted the top of her round belly.

His ears burned at the mention of the word *condom* and

he nearly dropped the toast he handed her. But he nodded, playing it cool.

"So," she said with a sigh. "You're hanging out for a few days?"

"Yeah. Mom will be back on Friday. How long are you staying?"

Jane went real still, her eyes glued to the toast she held halfway to her mouth. "Not long," she said.

"You gonna go home? To your mom and dad?"

She laughed but it wasn't funny. It was sad and mean at the same time. "Not likely," she said. "They're not too thrilled with me right now."

Spence thought of his mom yesterday morning, about how he'd been a little scared of her, and didn't know what to say.

With nothing else to do he put some more bread in the toaster and at the same time Jane's pocket rang and she dropped the toast like it was burning hot and dug out her phone.

Startled, Spence just watched as she looked at her screen and practically started to cry.

"Where are you?" she asked into the phone. "I'm totally freaking out." She jumped up from her stool and ran back to the rooms.

After a minute, when it was clear she wasn't coming right back, Spence reached out and grabbed her toast.

No sense in letting it go cold.

"You gonna spend the day in here?" Deb asked from the doorway of Sam's office.

"Well," Sam sighed. Her morning was slipping away on a

flood of sudden paperwork and she couldn't seem to stop it. "It wasn't my intention, but the accountant called saying there was an error on our grant application. I got that fixed. Then Alex called in sick and can't teach her résumé class and we've got six women coming in to take that class in—" she checked her watch "—a half hour and I can't find the damn handouts!" Sam slammed the desk drawer that didn't catch and bounced back to bang her knee. She slammed it again with the same result. She was about to slam it again when Deb put her hand on her shoulder.

"Stop," she said. "You got J.D. in room two and a boy out at that kitchen table and you're having a hissy fit in here."

After the revelations of last night she'd gotten about ten seconds of sleep. And just hearing J.D.'s name made her heart pound and her head hurt. And she knew Spence was out there, waiting for her, but she didn't know what to do with him. About him. For him.

She was emptied out. Hollow.

"I'm not having a hissy fit."

"Right. Because no one else can teach that résumé class, huh?" Deb asked, her hands on her hips. "No one else can find those handouts? And that accountant you pay the big bucks to can't fix a grant application?"

"I told him to contact me," Sam said. "It's policy."

"Policy." Deb shook her head. "It's policy that you do everything. I'm supposed to be your assistant and all I do is drive people to doctors' appointments."

"That's not true," Sam said, wondering what Deb was talking about. "You do so much."

"I do plenty of the things you tell me to do," Deb said and finally Sam gave up and sat down.

"What are you getting at, Deb?"

"I'm getting at the fact that it's policy that you do everything around here. Someone can't teach, you do it. Someone makes a mistake, you fix it. You don't let me help."

"You want to teach the class?"

Deb reached out and pulled Sam to her feet.

"Deb." Sam groaned. "What are—"

"Your son is out there," Deb said, giving Sam a little shake. "He's here, on his own to get to know you and you are locking yourself up in here. You got a man out there who keeps coming back to you for more and you are locking yourself up in here. You're hiding because this stuff—" she gestured to the cluttered boxes and the broken chair "—is easy for you."

"There's work—"

"There will always be work," Deb said. "Always. But you keep doing it and that's all there will be."

Sam's stomach did a free fall to her feet and she went slack in Deb's arms. This was easier. The doctors' appointments and bad plumbing and everyone else's problems were simpler.

Spence. J.D. Her life. Was so damn hard.

"Oh, no." She groaned and dropped her head down on Deb's shoulder.

"You're dumb but you're not stupid." Deb laughed, stroking her back.

"I just don't know what to do with him," Sam admitted.

"Spence or J.D.?"

"Either one of them," she said, wanting to cry.

"I'll teach that class. You go take your son out for a walk to the pond. Take a lunch. Take J.D. Go for a swim."

Really? she thought. *That works? It's that simple?*

"Trust me, sweetie," Deb said, reading her expression. "A cool swim on a hot day puts lots of things right."

"What would I do without you?" Sam asked, looking her friend right in the eye.

"Well, I'll tell you when my review comes up," Deb said and pushed her out the door, toward her son. Toward her life.

∾

J.D. HEARD Sam's voice coming around the side of the shelter and pulled his shirt out from where he'd tucked it in the back of his pants. Even covered in sweat and hotter than hell, he set down the old scythe and yanked the blue shirt over his head.

He didn't need to be any more naked in front of the woman.

He heard Spence's voice, then the higher-pitched tones of what had to be Christina Conti. Sam said something else and everyone laughed.

J.D. picked up the scythe and resumed attacking the ever-creeping kudzu vines. Grateful there was something here he could take a knife to.

"Hey, J.D.!" Spence yelled as they emerged from the side of the house. The boy took a few running steps toward him and then stopped. "What are you doing?"

"Cutting back the vines," he said, resting his elbow on the top of the scythe. He thought about what Sam had said, the way the boy had asked about him and felt guilt like stones roll through his stomach. "What are you up to?"

"We're going for a swim," Spence said, pointing down at a pair of cutoff jeans that showed off his bird legs. Something about those knees made J.D. smile.

"That's a pretty good thing to do on a day like today," he said, wiping at the sweat that stung his eyes.

"Why don't you come?" Spence asked, all lit up from the inside. "It'll be fun. Sam said there's a rope swing."

He knew about the rope swing. He'd climbed that big oak five years ago and tied the rope in place because, in his mind, every pond in the South should have something like that.

"I don't think so, Spence," he said, not even bothering to look at Sam. He rolled his shoulders and repositioned his grip on the old wooden handle. "I want to finish—"

"Come with us, J.D.," Sam said.

He met her gaze, surprised to find it so steadfast. Buried in those familiar brown eyes was an invitation and an understanding that made his skin too tight.

I told you, he thought, feeling his heart beat fast. *I told you what I am.*

"I want you to come," Sam said, unrelenting. Then, as if hearing her words she gestured to Spence who was bouncing. "We all do."

"Come on," Spence wheedled.

"It's way too hot to do anything else," Christina added, fanning her face with her hand.

He glanced at Sam again unable, really, to look away. He'd wondered what she'd say to him this morning. How, after a night's sleep, she'd come to her senses and ask him to leave, thank him for his time politely, but insist that things would be better without him there.

He'd expected that.

What he got was her beautiful face graced with a tentative smile.

"I packed ham sandwiches," she said, holding up a bag.

"Lots of them," Spence said. "Come on, come on."

J.D. was stuck, trapped in mud. Concrete.

"Please," she said, and his heart lurched.

"Well, if ham sandwiches are involved—" he said, giving up the fight. "I'll be right back."

He took the scythe to the shed and locked it, wondering what in the world he was getting into.

Sam led them down the narrow trail that was in grave danger of being eaten by kudzu and he brought up the rear, the two kids between them.

He imagined this was the way other families walked. Real families, going on trips. Doing family things.

Not a family, he reminded himself. Sam's optimistic insanity must be spreading.

"Hey, J.D.," Spence said, turning to walk backward.

"Careful, kid," J.D. said. "You could trip."

"I won't." Then he did.

J.D. fought back a smile and helped Spence up. "You all right?"

"Fine," Spence said, shaking the dirt off his shorts. "Can I ask you some questions?"

"I guess," J.D. said tentatively.

"Do you have a history of cancer in your family?"

Sam's laugh brought them both up short. "What's so funny?" J.D. asked Sam, who had stopped and was looking at them over her shoulder. Her smile was wide, her eyes bright, her hair a wild pile on her head and he felt his throat constrict.

"You'll see," Sam said and winked at Spence. She started walking again.

"Do you?" Spence asked.

"Nope."

"Heart disease?"

"What is this, kid?"

"Just a couple of questions."

Good God, in the fifteen minutes it took to get to the pond, J.D. gave the most thorough medical history he'd ever given. Spence seemed a bit bummed that there wasn't more life-threatening heart disease running rampant in his genes and J.D. was tempted to make some stuff up to give the kid a thrill.

But they finally broke through the woods to the small hilltop around the pond.

"There's no beach," Christina said, sounding peeved and out of breath.

"Where's the rope swing?" Spence said, practically plowing into Sam.

"Here," he said, moving on ahead of Sam, who was looking at the pond as though she'd never seen it before. "You've got to walk to the other side. There's a little clearing. Not much of a beach. And the rope swing is tied to that big oak over there." He leaned down and pointed to the tree across the pond, nestled up next to an eroded section of the bank.

"Let's go," Spence said, hopping on ahead. Christina groaned and followed.

Which left him standing next to Sam.

"I haven't been here in years," she said.

"Five years?" he asked, thinking of that night tying the rope to the tree and making love in the water.

"I guess so," she murmured, shaking her head. "There's something wrong with that, isn't there?" she asked. "I live right here and never find a chance to go swimming?" Her brown eyes seemed baffled, as though she was figuring something out.

"You're asking the wrong guy," he said. "I'm no authority

on what's right." He stepped forward to catch up with the kids and she grabbed his arm.

"J.D.," she said, and the contact of her sweaty palm on his forearm zinged through his body.

"We need to talk," she said. "About—"

"No, we don't," he said, stepping away from her touch, not wanting to talk about it at all. "I'm not one of the women in your shelter, Sam," he said, looking right at her, hoping she got it. Needing her to get it. Needing her to leave him be. "I'm no victim of circumstance. There's nothing more to the story. I am what I am."

J.D. took off toward the kids because he had to get away from Sam, from her bleeding heart and easy forgiveness.

"How does this work?" Spence asked, holding the frayed end of the thick rope.

"Well," Sam said, not at all sure how the rope swing worked and all too aware of J.D. behind her. Everything in her was hypertuned to him, hyperaware. She felt his gaze like a touch, could feel his breath, the hot air he moved when he walked past her. She could smell him—sweat and J.D.—a combination that used to knock her right off her feet. She was a little dismayed to see that it still did.

He was a brick wall. Unwilling to talk, casting off her pathetic efforts to help like she meant nothing.

Maybe they'd done too much harm to each other. Lied too often. Perhaps there was no way for him to see past what he'd done as a kid. Who was she to think that she could change him. Now? It was ridiculous.

"Don't you just hold on to the knot?" she asked, turning slightly to J.D., not wanting to look directly at him because it hurt so much to see him standing right there, but seeming a million miles away.

His lip quirked. "You really haven't been out here," he said and stepped forward to take over the instructions. "You stand on the knot."

Spence turned white at that, looking down past the edge of the embankment they stood on to the water below.

"It's really easy," J.D. said.

"What if I fall?"

"You won't," J.D. insisted. "You hold on until you get over the water and then you let go."

Spence still wasn't sold and Sam smiled. Feeling like a third wheel, she walked back to the dirt beach where Christina sat.

"How you feeling?" Sam asked the girl, dropping the backpack of lunch next to the fallen log the girl was sitting on.

"Like a whale," Christina said, drawing stars in the dirt with a stick. "But it's good to walk around. The baby seems to like it," she said with a small smile, pressing a hand to the side of her belly.

"Wait until you go swimming," Sam said. "When I was pregnant, I went to a pool in town once and Spence—" She felt that strange sensation of her world shrinking. In her mind, she'd been pregnant and there was Spence; the two weren't entirely the same thing. But now every detail of the pregnancy flooded her and she was struck dumb by the stupid simple realization that it had been Spence kicking her. "Spence loved it," she whispered.

"Are you sad you gave him up?" Christina asked.

Sam sucked a deep breath. "I don't really know how to answer that," she said honestly. "Yes and no, maybe. I never thought about it before he came here to visit. But it's obvious I made the right choice."

"You think?" the girl asked, her eyebrows crinkling in teenage disbelief.

"Yeah." Sam nodded. "He's had a rough go of it lately, but his dad loved him. His mom loves him. He's smart and cared for and as much as he's curious about J.D. and me, it's obvious who he belongs with."

Christina went back to drawing, changing her subject material from stars to houses, and suddenly Sam realized what the girl was really asking.

"Are you thinking of giving your baby up for adoption?" she asked and Christina stopped drawing but didn't look up.

"I'm sixteen," she whispered and Sam nearly fell off the log. "My boyfriend is seventeen. And I just don't think we can handle it. I mean—" She sighed. "I thought we could, but since we told my parents, everything has gotten so weird. You know?"

More than you know, sweetheart.

"Do you think it's time to call your parents?" Sam asked, because now that the girl had admitted her age, Sam had a responsibility. "They must be freaking out."

"I'm sure my mom is," Christina said, wiping the side of her face on the shoulder of her T-shirt. "When I left..." Her bottom lip trembled before she bit it. "I miss my mom."

Policy dictated Sam hike Christina back to the shelter right now to contact her parents. Sam looked up at the sun then over at Spence and J.D. at the tree and again at the girl beside her. Policy had dictated too much for her. A few hours in the sunshine would do all of them some good. "Maybe we should give them a call later," Sam said, stroking the girl's shoulder. "Maybe that would make you feel better."

Christina just sat there, every muscle tense as if she would break with an inhale.

"Breathe, honey," Sam said. "You've got to breathe."

Christina's breath hitched and she smiled briefly and wiped her eyes.

Sam watched J.D. wave his arms out over the pond as if showing Spence the mechanics of swinging.

"Are you going to have more kids?" Christina asked.

The world tipped under her or maybe she was floating, watching everything from a distance, from suddenly so far away.

Across the water J.D. hung his head, then took off his shirt and kicked off his boots. Spence hooted and J.D. wrapped his hands around the rope, every muscle along his back flexing and shifting under skin that gleamed like copper. He took off, arching over the water and at the height of the swing, as all his momentum slowed, he let go, falling backward in the water with a tremendous splash.

Spence cheered from the banks as if J.D. had just saved the free world. When the rope swung back to him, the boy reached out, his thin white arms stretched wide and he grabbed for the rope, but missed, nearly falling in the water.

J.D. laughed and splashed him.

I'm a fool.

Thinking she had a choice about loving J.D.?

It simply was, like breathing. Like this pond and their son. Her feelings were a truth. A reality.

She loved J.D.

"Do you want more kids?" Christina asked again.

"Yes," Sam whispered, finding the truth without having to search. It was simply there, floating on top of everything, so light it was no wonder she'd never realized it was there before.

SAM CALLED everyone to the fallen log for ham sandwiches and J.D. stretched out beside her in soaking-wet jeans and bare feet.

He was so gorgeous. So sexual to her that she thought maybe she should shield Christina's eyes, but the teenager didn't seem to notice.

Everything in Sam started to hum at the sight of damp denim clinging to muscles. She wanted to peel those pants off him, dry him with her skin.

Her feelings were raw with her new understanding of how tied she was to J.D. To feel so much for him and to be so unsure of how he truly felt about her made her slightly dizzy. Slightly sick to her stomach.

"Hey," Spence said, taking a ham sandwich, and Sam jerked her eyes away from J.D., her cheeks on fire. "Can I ask some more questions?"

Everyone, even Christina, groaned.

"No," Sam said, looking at the boy, happy for a good distraction from J.D.'s appeal. "You can't. I want to ask you some questions."

Spence blinked at her then shrugged. "Shoot."

"What's your favorite color?" she asked.

"Green," Spence said.

"Mine, too," J.D. said and ate a third of his sandwich in one bite.

"It is?" she asked, shocked. Green, really? She had him pegged as more of a black fan. Maybe blue.

He shrugged and leaned against the log. "It's a nice color."

"Okay," she said, thinking. "What's your favorite subject in school?"

"Social studies," Spence answered and her heart sparked. That had been hers, too, all the way into college. "This is fun, ask more."

"Favorite TV show?"

"*The Simpsons.*"

"Oh," Christina said, "I love that show."

"Favorite food?" Sam asked.

"Fried mushrooms," he said.

"Gross," J.D. said, wrinkling his nose.

"No, it's not." Spence laughed, smacking J.D. in the shoulder. "My dad and I used to eat them all the time."

"Well," J.D. said, "that's nice. But it's still gross."

"What's yours?" Spence asked.

"Ham sandwiches," J.D. and Sam said at the same time. Everyone laughed, while Sam avoided J.D.'s eyes.

Everyone went back to their sandwiches, taking sips from pop cans that had grown warm in the heat.

Christina started tossing rocks into the water and Spence joined her, trying to throw them farther, without much luck.

Sam wiggled her toes in the damp dirt and felt everything in her brain go quiet. This was one of those perfect moments. Slightly strange, she thought, looking at her former lover with the terrifying past, their son, loaned out to them for four days, and the pregnant mafia princess who somehow rounded out the group.

Sam started to smile and caught J.D.'s eyes, where she saw a similar humor sparkling.

"No one would believe us if we told them," he said to her and she laughed, loving that he'd practically read her mind.

"Believe what?" Spence asked, chucking a big fat sinker into the pond.

"The question I have for you," J.D. said, changing the

subject with total grace. "If you could have any superpower, what would it be?" he asked.

"Oh, that's a good one," Spence said and crouched in the dirt to think.

"I'd read people's minds," Sam said. God, wouldn't her life be easier then. She'd know the rest of J.D.'s story, she'd know what he was thinking as he watched her from that log, his eyes hooded, his face serious.

"I'd be invisible," Christina said.

"I was going to say that," Spence groused.

"You can have the same power," Sam said.

"No, we can't," Spence said and Sam wondered when the rules had been established. "Oh, I know. I'd fly. Wouldn't that be awesome?"

"Totally awesome," J.D. agreed.

"What's yours?" Spence asked, all damp, eager puppy.

"I'd fly, too," J.D. said.

"Can't be the same as mine, you have to pick another one."

J.D. tossed the rest of his sandwich toward the trees, where it was quickly snapped up by squirrels. "I'd be able to go back in time."

Spence's face screwed up. "And do what?" He clearly didn't understand the cool factor of J.D.'s power. But Sam understood and the significance almost paralyzed her.

"I'd fix things," J.D. said, his eyes boring a hole right through Sam.

12

"I'm going to bed," Christina whispered, waking up from where she'd fallen asleep on the couch twenty minutes ago.

J.D. nodded and watched the girl shuffle out of the common room. Spence was passed out cold against J.D., his head against his ribs. Sam was curled up and lightly snoring in the big chair while *The Incredibles* just got good and the pizza got cold on the floor in front of them.

What a day, J.D. thought, staring blindly at the cartoon flickering in the dark room. The kind of day he never thought he'd have again. Not that he'd had them when he was a kid, but in the past ten years, every day he'd had with Sam had felt this way.

A day playing hooky.

Spence rearranged himself and J.D. shifted his arm so the kid lay flat on the couch, his head resting against J.D.'s thigh.

Holding his breath, he pressed his hand to the boy's red curls.

What a day.

"What time is it?" Sam's sleepy, rough voice reached out through the dark and stroked J.D.'s skin, went right to his bloodstream the way it always did.

How many times had he called her late at night from someplace, just to hear her sleepy voice across the miles that separated them. Just so he could feel close to her. Not many was the answer. Things had to be really bad for him to give himself that kind of treat.

"About eleven," he answered, being careful to keep his eyes on the TV screen. He knew what she would look like, rosy and stretching like a cat in that chair, her delicate body uncoiling.

He heard her yawn and groan a little. "Wow," she finally said. "It's late. I should—" She stopped. "Wake him up? I guess? I don't think I can carry him."

"I can carry him upstairs," he volunteered. *I can carry him upstairs*, he thought. *Into those dark, rose-scented rooms. I can put him to bed then crawl under your covers and we can end this perfect day right.*

"That would be great," she said and turned off the television, plunging the room into sudden blackness. It took a moment for his eyes to adjust but there was plenty of moonlight streaming in the big front window.

Enough that he could see Sam.

And want her more than he should.

His whole body started to ache, like a fever had him. And not surprisingly, after the day they'd had, he wasn't angry about it. He wasn't angry about her. Carrying his son upstairs and wanting her seemed about the two most right things in the world.

He stood and bent over the couch, scooping his arms under Spence, who rolled easily toward him.

"Light as a feather," J.D. told Sam, catching her worried expression as she stood at the open door to her apartment.

He didn't think about the boy's implicit trust or the way it seemed to knit certain parts of him back together. He didn't think about how forgiving Sam for not telling him about Spence settled into place without any effort on his part.

He didn't think about any of it. He just held the boy close and thanked God that he had a chance to do this just once in his sorry life.

Sam's quarters were stuffy and she went around the room cracking open windows and flicking on the ceiling fan while he laid the boy on the fold-out couch. J.D. eased off Spence's shoes and slid his feet under the blue-and-white cloud sheets Sam had put on the bed.

And then, knowing she was there, watching him, waiting for him, her need to talk like a low pressure zone in the room, he stood and met her eyes.

A moment passed and they said nothing. They just were.

"It was a good day," she said. "I'm glad you came."

He smiled and tucked his hands into his pockets. "I'm glad you made me go."

Her eyes searched his in the moonlight. Damp and glowing, they dug deep looking for something in him that would make what she wanted okay.

She wouldn't find it. And she would try to twist something out of the nothing inside him.

"Go to bed, Sam," he whispered.

She shook her head.

He felt her intentions like fingers reaching for him and he held up his hand.

"Sam," he said, warning clear in his voice. "I don't know

what you intend to do, but if you come closer...we won't be talking."

She stopped, blinked at him.

Stepped forward.

"Be sure," he whispered. "Be really sure, Sam. Because I'm not who you thought I was."

"I know who you are," she said. "I've known who you are from the day you stepped into this shelter. I may not have known what you've done. I may not have known your real name, but I know you."

Air churned in his lungs, his flesh was swollen, on fire for her. He couldn't think past his need to let her touch him.

"I know you, J.D.," she whispered, stepping so close her breasts hit his chest and he hissed at the contact. "And you are a good man."

With her, he was. He watched her hands reach for him, unable to breathe as he waited. With her he was a better man.

Then she touched him, her fingers slipping under the sleeve of his T-shirt, and his skin twitched with delight. Her eyes burned into his and even if the house exploded he wouldn't have been able to look away from her.

Her hands traced the ridge of his bicep, curled under his arm, traced a vein down to his forearms, then laced her fingers through his, joining them.

"I want to sleep with you," she whispered, lifting their hands to press kisses to his knuckles, the tips of his fingers. "But I can't do it if you are still angry with me about keeping Spence a secret."

"I'm not," he said.

She smiled sadly, licking his thumb then biting it. "Are you saying that so I'll have sex with you?"

He shook his head. "I'm saying it because it's true. I can't judge you for how you acted in that situation."

She closed her eyes and a tear slid down her cheek. He groaned at the sight, clenching his hands to hers, bringing them to his chest. His lips.

"I forgive you for not telling me your real name," she said.

He shook his head. "Don't," he told her. "I don't deserve that."

Her beautiful, baffled eyes met his. "Yes, you do. You—"

The pressure in him built until it burst, forcing him into action. He pushed his hands into the silk of her hair and kissed her.

To distract her, to shut her up. Because today had been one of the best days of his life and it was killing him to not kiss her.

She jerked as if filled by an electric current, then she moaned, deep in her chest, and kissed him back.

Her hands curled over his biceps, holding him close, her fingernails tiny pinpricks of pain and heat that he adored.

He relished the way her lips pressed back, opened, let him in. The way her tongue touched his, her teeth scraped his lips. Funny how he never really thought about the way Sam kissed; it was all part of the package. But this kiss, he focused on wholly. Memorizing the taste and feel of her.

His hands fisted her hair, and she vibrated against him. He eased back far enough to see her eyes. He wanted to drink her down. He didn't have the strength to deny himself anymore. To deny her. If she pushed, he'd shatter.

So he didn't give either one of them a chance to say no, to change their minds, to come to their senses.

He kissed her again, sweeping her up in his arms.

The darkness was no hindrance. He knew his way to

Sam's bed from across the country and he carried her there, never lifting his lips from hers.

The bedroom door clicked shut behind them and he felt as if it was all a dream, a dream he'd had a million times, that he would wake up from, hard and lonely and desperate.

Her body slid to the ground, but never lost contact with his and somehow in his efforts to get her naked, his own clothes fell off and soon it was her beautiful silky bare skin pressed to his.

His hands slid over her, from her strong shoulders, down her breasts, over her thin waist to the firm curve of her butt. He cupped her hips in his hands and lifted and pushed her harder against him, his erection jerking against her.

It was too fast, too much. He wanted to go slow, treasure her. Worship her for hours.

He eased her onto the bed, helping her scramble over the quilt until just her feet dangled off the edge of the bed.

She was like some kind of sex-goddess fantasy, lying across that bed, her red hair spilled around her. Her eyes half shut, her lips wet.

He leaned forward to touch the hardened tip of her breast. She undulated against his hand and he liked that so much that he pinched her, just a little, just like she loved and her legs spread against his, trapping him between her knees.

"You're so beautiful," he whispered, falling down on his hands over her body. He licked her other nipple and she groaned, twisting again, so he used his teeth.

"Now," she demanded. "Come on."

Her hand slipped between their bodies and gripped his erection. He dropped his head to her shoulder, watching her hand on him, unable to breathe.

She stroked him, base to tip and back again. Her thumb

circled the head, caught the clear drop at the tip and she brought it to her lips.

He realized every minute he didn't spend in bed with this woman was a total waste of time. Pushing off his hands, he fell to his knees on the floor and cupped his hands under her hips, dragging her closer to him, to the edge.

"J.D." His name was a gasp as his lips touched her, his fingers found her and he just settled in. The muscles along his spine, in his belly, relaxed and he curved over her. He pushed away his own raging desire, the erection that throbbed with its own heartbeat. He turned off every noise but those she made. He turned off his doubts, his second-guesses, his demons and his fears.

He let himself go and focused on the woman under his hands and the love he had for her pounding in his heart.

SPENCE JERKED awake at the sound of a man and woman laughing. For a second he forgot where he was and what had happened and he thought it was Mom and Dad. It was Sunday morning, the best mornings, when Mom made French toast and Dad would clear off the breakfast table and do a puzzle with him all morning.

He rolled over on his back, his eyes closed and he could smell the French toast, the bacon, the bitter burn of his parents' coffee. He thought of which puzzle they'd do today, maybe the New York City one. It was so hard it would take most of the day. That way Dad wouldn't go into his office and check e-mail and not come out for hours.

"Shh, J.D. You're going to wake him."

J.D.? And the woman didn't sound like his mom and

slowly the dream began to fade. His sheets felt different and that sweet French toast smell was actually flowery.

This isn't my home, he realized, coming out of the dream.

"It's okay, Sam," J.D. whispered. "He's still sleeping. I'll be really quiet."

And that's not my dad, Spence thought. He was at Sam's house and it was J.D. going into the kitchen making coffee.

He rolled over onto his side, squeezing his eyes shut against the burning hot tears.

SAM'S GIDDINESS was tempered by a real fear of the unknown. She lay in bed, J.D.'s hands stroking her belly, his fingers tracing the scar, and she wondered, couldn't help but wonder, what's next?

The words hammered at her teeth, dying to come out, so she kept her jaw clamped. In all their years together, she'd never felt this way—this worried and desperate about their future. It seemed, in those years, that she'd come to convince herself that not knowing was the point. Not knowing was what she wanted.

Now she could barely stand to look at him, naked and rumpled in her bed, fiercely masculine, stupidly sexy against her silly sheets.

Drinking coffee like nothing had changed.

When Christina had asked her yesterday if she wanted kids, it had been easy to say yes. But looking at J.D., Sam realized the hard part was that she wanted *his* kids.

She wanted him.

Suddenly, she was suffocated by all she didn't know and all she wanted. She parted her lips to breathe, and the words began to tumble out.

"J.D., what does—"

Downstairs, Daisy started barking and they both sat up.

"It's probably Christina," J.D. said, reaching for his pants anyway. "Going to the kitchen or something."

"Right," Sam answered. She wanted to believe him, but guard dogs barked because something was wrong. And Daisy was a guard dog. She rolled out of bed and grabbed her robe, swinging it around her shoulders.

They crept out of the bedroom, but it was too late. Spence was already awake, his hair sticking up in a wild rooster tail on the back of his head.

"What's wrong?" Spence asked, sitting in a puddle of blue-and-white sheets, his little body tense with nerves.

"Nothing, kiddo," J.D. said, rumpling his hair. "But I'm going to go downstairs and check on Daisy. She probably saw a squirrel outside."

Sam was right behind J.D., despite his stern look indicating his disapproval.

"My dog," she grumbled. "My shelter."

He jogged down the stairs, not even pausing when his phone rang. Digging it out of his pocket, he opened the door to the kitchen and Sam raced around him while he answered the phone.

J.D. grabbed the edge of her robe, but she jerked free. She didn't need protecting, not in her own home.

Daisy was in the common room, her front paws against the glass, barking like mad at a totally empty street.

"What's got into you?" she whispered, pulling Daisy off the window only to have her lunge back up. "Jeez, Louise, dog, cool it. There's nothing out there."

Her surging heart rate slowly started beating normally and she led her squirrel-hunting dog back into the kitchen.

J.D. was nowhere to be found and her office door was

shut and so she decided to check in on Christina, who had to be dead asleep to be able to ignore the episode of Dumb Animal Kingdom outside her door.

"Jane?" she said, knocking lightly on the closed door of the girl's room. When there was no answer she knocked harder and the unlocked door swung open slightly.

Weird, Sam thought, the girl was so fierce about her privacy. Sam stepped into the dark room. "Jane?"

The window shades were pulled and Sam could just make out the girl's body under the covers on the bed.

Sam thought about leaving, letting the girl sleep, but Daisy started to growl low and deep in her throat.

A breeze blew through the room from the open window and Sam's skin went cold.

Something was very, very wrong here.

She reached out to the bed, her hand shaking and when she pressed on the covers, they deflated. She patted down the whole bed and the mounds she thought had been girl-shaped were just an unmade bed.

Empty. No Christina.

She ran to the bathroom and it, too, was empty.

Oh, no. Oh, no.

Daisy was barking. Growling, leaping around her feet.

She ran back to Christina's room and flipped on the light. Something glimmered on the table and she grabbed it.

Her heart plummeted. It was the diamond ring the girl wore around her neck with a note under it.

Thank you, it said, in Christina's curly handwriting. And *I'm sorry*.

The note crumpled in Sam's suddenly sweaty fist. The girl ran? Was it possible? Did her dad pick her up? Realization struck. The boyfriend. The boyfriend who had been heading here.

She spun, heading back through the house for J.D.

The kitchen was empty, her office door open and she found him in the common room, about to open the front door.

"J.D.," she cried. "Christina's gone."

"Gone?" For a second a panic so profound hit J.D.'s face and seeing it made her own pulse skyrocket. She put a hand over her heart as if to stroke it into a tempo more bearable. "What do you mean?"

"Her room is empty, her window is open and I found this." She held out the ring and the note and J.D. snatched it from her hands.

He swore under his breath.

"Sam," he whispered. "This is bad news."

"No kidding," she said. "The girl is six months pregnant and sixteen years old." She should have marched Christina right back to the house yesterday, once the girl had confessed her age. She should have followed policy. Maybe then they wouldn't be in this mess. "Oh, I totally screwed up," she muttered. And that little girl was paying for it. Running around like some kind of fugitive.

"It's worse than that," J.D. said, handing Sam the ring. "Greg just called me and early this morning Conti and his wife went to New York City to talk to their oldest girl, then they headed south."

"South?" Sam asked as J.D. took a gun from the back waistband of his pants and checked the chambers.

"What are you doing with a gun?" she asked, cool sweat gathering along her spine. This whole thing was suddenly surreal. It had to be a dream. A bad one, but one she'd wake up from any moment.

The doorbell rang and Daisy went nuts at her side and Sam reached down to hold on to her collar.

"I need you to go upstairs and stay up there," J.D. said, pulling on a T-shirt he must have grabbed when he grabbed his gun from his stuff in room two.

"Why?" she asked. She jerked her chin toward the door, holding Daisy back with both hands. "Who's here?"

"Just go—"

The doorbell rang again.

"Who is at the door?"

J.D. looked through the peephole and swore before resting his head against the door.

"Francis Conti," he answered.

13

Sam was being stupidly stubborn and it made J.D. frantic to knock her out and carry her caveman style to some safer cave.

"Go upstairs. Keep Spence there."

"Don't be ridiculous," she snapped, keeping her voice low as though Conti could hear them. "This is my home."

"It's a shelter, Sam," J.D. barked, his temper, his sanity all fraying. "It's four rooms above a damn women's shelter. That's not a home. It's an apartment and a job. For God's sake, just be smart about this."

She blinked at him and he knew he'd hurt her, wounded her someplace soft and vulnerable, but he couldn't care about that right now. All he cared about was that Frank Conti was here, looking for a daughter who wasn't here. And there was no telling what that would result in.

"Think of Spence," he said, playing the guilt card. "He's going to be scared by himself."

"He's hardly here to murder us," Sam said, looking far too feminine in her robe, far too appealing to be in the same room as the monster Conti. "Don't you think you're overreacting?"

"Overreacting?" he asked, and stepped closer to Sam, his hands gripping her shoulders hard enough to leave bruises. "This man is a killer, Sam. A murderer. You don't know him—"

"You don't either."

He shook her. "My father was this guy. I would have been this guy. I know who he is down to his socks and I don't want you in the same room as him. I don't want you in the same room as me right now."

"Open the door, J.D.," she said, strong as she'd ever been. "He's here to see me."

"At least go change—"

Sam reached forward and, before he could stop her, she'd unlocked the door and jerked it open.

J.D.'s worst nightmare stood on the porch. A tall man, dark and thin, with that unfortunate nose, looking ready to tear apart the world at the slightest provocation.

And worse, he was sweating yet still wearing a leather coat in the hot summer morning.

J.D.'s blood ran cold.

He barely noticed the round blond woman with the tear-streaked face mostly covered by big black sunglasses beside him.

Daisy went nuts, broke free of Sam's grasp and lunged toward Conti. Conti stepped back, protecting his wife and reached inside his jacket with his right hand just as J.D. collared the dog.

That the man came armed was confirmed.

"What kind of place is this?" the blonde whispered, looking close to a meltdown.

"Sorry about that," Sam said, managing to sound as normal as can be, while J.D. could barely see straight with nerves and worry. His heart was never going to work right again. "Daisy is our guard dog and she takes her job very seriously."

Conti's hands spread wide in mild surrender and J.D. realized he had one hand on the dog and the other hand behind his back on the butt of his gun.

"You can call off both your dogs," Francis said, watching J.D. from the corner of his eye.

"We're looking for our little girl," his wife said. "I'm Carmen Conti and this is my husband, Frank. Our oldest daughter told us that Christina might be here."

"Of course," Sam said. Her gaze flickered to J.D.'s and she stepped out onto the porch. "We can talk out here. We have some kids sleeping inside."

Well, he thought, at least she wasn't a total fool.

"Could you take Daisy to my office?" Sam asked J.D., and he shot her an incredulous look. As if he was going to leave her alone with a murderer. "You are making things worse," she whispered as the Contis watched them.

The guy was like a black cancer, all wrong in a place so good. It was the way he'd always felt about himself. Like the man he was, really was, shouldn't be in a place like this. It wasn't right. And seeing this thug, his black leather coat gleaming like an oil slick, J.D. knew he was right.

But J.D. could see that he and Daisy, growling low in her throat, were indeed making things worse. And worse wasn't what anyone needed.

So he ran the dog to the office and practically threw her in. The dog's claws scrambled against the cracked linoleum and finally gained purchase. She shifted her massive weight and went charging back for the door, but J.D. slammed it shut and headed out through the common room to the front lawn.

He was going to kill Greg, that's for sure. Calling him ten minutes before Conti showed up? What kind of warning was that? If J.D. had had a half hour, he would have been able to get Sam and the kid out of here. Well, maybe not, given Sam's foolish resolve, but he would have had a chance.

"Can I get you anything?" Sam asked, practically glowing in the early morning sunlight.

"We're fine," Conti snapped and J.D. wanted to take the guy's eyes out for using that tone with Sam. "We're just looking for our Tina."

Carmen held out a photo and Sam took it, glancing at it with a smile.

"Your daughter was here," Sam said and Mrs. Conti put a hand out, bracing herself on her husband.

"Oh, thank God," she breathed, crossing herself.

"What do you mean, was?" Francis asked, his eyebrows snapping together.

Sam licked her lips and J.D. kept an eye on Conti's right hand, ready for anything. Ready for the worst.

"She showed up on Friday afternoon." Sam conducted herself like a businesswoman despite wearing a robe and being barefoot. "She said her name was Jane Doe and that she was twenty-one."

"Was she still pregnant?" Carmen asked.

Sam nodded. "She is still pregnant."

Again, Carmen crossed herself, tears rolling down her face.

J.D. saw the edge of a black bruise under her sunglasses and his gut went colder.

"We got her a doctor's appointment and the baby is healthy. Christina is, too. A little too thin, but the doctor said she was carrying the baby just fine."

"What do you mean, was here?" Francis asked again, his voice harder, his tone uglier. J.D. stepped in closer, letting the guy know that just because the dog was gone, didn't mean there wasn't a guard.

"When we woke up this morning she was gone," Sam said and held out the note and the ring. "She left these."

Carmen's hands shook as she took the objects from Sam's hands. Francis started pacing, muttering under his breath, throwing off anger like a cold wind.

J.D. took deep breaths, trying not to add to the tension. Conti was the worst kind of loose cannon and J.D. did not want to give the lunatic a reason to take out all that barely controlled rage on Sam or the shelter.

"So you...do you know where she is?" Carmen asked.

Sam shook her head. "I don't—"

"What kind of place is this?" Conti snapped. "You let a sixteen-year-old pregnant girl come and go in the middle of the night?"

"I need you to calm down," J.D. said, stepping between Sam and Francis.

"This isn't any of your business," Conti said, menace rolling off him in waves. He put his hands on his hips, fanning his jacket out, showing off the butt of the gun tucked into his pants. His eyes were wild and he was looking for an excuse to bust something up.

"Francis," Carmen said.

"Shut up, Carm." Francis leaned around J.D. and pointed a finger at his wife. "We've done this whole thing your way. We've given the stupid girl time to come to her senses and we've treated her like an adult. And look where it's gotten us." He held out his hands, his laugh ridiculing. "Some crappy women's shelter in the middle of nowhere. And we still don't have her. If we'd—"

"Perhaps it's time you and I stepped away," J.D. said, his voice quiet, but strong as a punch and Conti's head snapped back to him.

"Who the hell are you?" Conti said, measuring him.

"I'm here to make sure you don't make a tough situation worse," J.D. said.

"Worse?" Conti spat, his eyes boring into J.D.'s. and J.D. braced himself. It was only a matter of time. "Wait a second." Conti blinked. "I know you, don't I?"

"I'm J. D. Kronos," he said.

Conti's eyes split wide and his mouth fell open. "What the hell? The butcher's boy?"

J.D. tightened his jaw and didn't say anything.

Conti started laughing and the sound of it was so close to the sound of his father's mean laugh that something in his belly trembled. Something angry and scared at the same time.

"He's a friend," Sam interjected, fiercely like Daisy at the door.

"You need better friends," Conti said. "Do you know what this guy did to his own father?" J.D. stepped forward intending to haul the man away so he could wipe that grin off the guy's face. Conti must have read his intentions because his body tensed. His eyes got hard.

"Where's your bat?" Conti asked, his chin out just begging for a left hook that would drop him.

"We're getting off topic," Sam said, stepping between them. J.D. reached out and pulled her away from Conti.

The guy's black eyes tracked the movement, saw everything. He smiled and all the man's evil filled the air like smoke.

"Don't like her near me, huh?" he asked. "It's not like you're any different. You look just like your dad, you know. And that guy was always ready for a fight, too."

J.D. felt the poison, the poison of his father's temper seep into him. He wanted to kill this guy. His hands were fists and he was ready to show Conti just how much of the butcher pounded through his veins.

"J.D.?" Spence's voice shook from the open front door and J.D. felt the world stop spinning.

Oh, God. Spence stood there, one sock missing, his hair a mess.

How many times had J.D. watched his father charge across a room to beat some guy senseless? How many times had he heard his father arguing with someone only to listen to it all end in screams and the sickening thuds of fists hitting soft tissue?

Here he was about to do the same thing. In front of his boy.

J.D. was no different. None. The proof was right here. Bringing violence into Serenity? In front of his son?

What is wrong with me? he wondered, sick to his stomach.

"What's going on?" Spence asked.

"Nothing, Spence." Sam was over at the boy before J.D. could get his bearings. Conti's eyes looked at the boy then glanced up at him.

"Those eyes are familiar," he said, knowing and mocking.

J.D. leaned forward, unable to control himself. "Don't even look at him," he whispered. "Or I'll take your eyes out."

"Francis!" Carmen cried.

"Shut up, Carmen. I swear to God—" Francis stepped toward Carmen and J.D. put himself in the way, stopping Conti like a brick wall. Conti's lips curled and his hands fisted and, even though J.D. knew Spence was watching, maybe because Spence was watching and he was so damn scared, J.D. grabbed the guy's jacket.

"Take a breath, Frank," he whispered.

"Gentlemen, please." Sam's voice rang out like a gunshot. "I will call the police."

The moment stretched, the panic in him grew until finally Frank blinked, his evil brown eyes regaining a little sanity. He held up his hands, stepped away and J.D. did the same thing. The cops wouldn't be good for anyone. Both men turned to Sam; her anger was palpable and frankly, considering the situation, shaming.

His son was watching. Their daughter was missing.

J.D. stepped away, farther and farther until he wasn't a part of the scene. His back was close to the house and he wished he could step right out off the earth.

Right out of his own skin.

Sam whispered something to Spence and tried to send him inside, but he shook his head, clinging to her hand. Sam shot J.D. a pleading look, begging him to help her. To take the boy inside.

His gut screamed no. Conti was still half-cocked and unpredictable.

"Take care of your son," Frank Conti said, his voice measured. Calm.

J.D. walked up to Spence. He held out his hand and the boy flinched, fear turning his skin white. His lips blue.

Spence was scared of him.

J.D. crouched, getting as close as the kid seemed to want

to let him. "I won't hurt you," J.D. whispered, feeling as if he'd aged a million years in the past ten minutes.

"You were going to hit that guy," Spence whispered and J.D. wished he could deny it. Wished he could have saved the kid having to see that. But it would have been a lie. He was who he was, no more running from it. Even at Serenity eventually his blood ran true.

"He's not a very nice guy," J.D. murmured.

"My dad said you should never hit anyone, ever. No matter how mean. Hitting people never makes anything better."

J.D. scrubbed at his face, pushing his hands through his hair. "Your dad was a smart guy," he said and looked at the boy, knowing it was over. Knowing the boy would never trust him again, nor should he. "Do you want to go upstairs now?"

Spence watched him, those old eyes freaking him out, seeing way more than any nine-year-old should.

"I can go by myself," Spence said, turning and walking up the stairs alone, leaving J.D. shattered.

Broken.

"I DON'T KNOW where your daughter has gone," Sam said, trying to pull her attention away from the whispered conversation J.D. and Spence were having. "But I am fairly sure she's with her boyfriend."

"That little shit?" Francis scowled and Carmen looked heavenward. Sam really wished the woman would take off those sunglasses—she had a bad feeling about what was being hidden behind those dark lenses.

"They can't be far," Sam said. "They left sometime late last night or early this morning."

"I'll find her," J.D. said, stepping close. "I can have her back to you by the end of the day."

"What?" she whispered. She was not entirely sure Christina was better off with her parents. Her father looked all too ready to beat the girl, as he probably had his wife. "Shouldn't we contact the authorities?"

"No need," J.D. said without looking at her, his eyes instead riveted to the vulturelike stare of Conti. "We don't want the authorities involved in this, do we?"

Conti's eye narrowed and he shook his head. "No," he said carefully. "We don't."

"Good. I can find her," J.D. said. "For a fee."

Conti laughed. "Well, it looks like you took up a different branch of the family business. Wouldn't Milo be proud."

"Do you want your daughter or not?" J.D. said, and Sam reached out to stall him, but he jerked away from her hand.

Sam stared at him, stunned. What was going on?

"Carmen." Conti held out his hand without ever looking at his wife. "Give me that ring."

Carmen's hands shook as she handed over the diamond.

"This should cover any costs," Conti said.

Sam watched, stunned and sick to her stomach as J.D. appraised the ring and dropped it in his pocket. "Do you have a number I can reach you?"

"What are you doing?" Sam asked, but J.D. ignored her.

"Yes," Conti said and again he held out a hand to his wife. "You have paper and a pencil in that suitcase you carry?" he asked and she fumbled through her bag.

The sunglasses slipped and the bruise around Carmen's eye was clearly visible. Oh, God. Oh, God. What was happening here?

Conti wrote down some numbers and handed the paper to J.D., holding on to J.D.'s hand a moment longer than necessary. "Don't blow this," he said, all kinds of threat in his voice. "Not like that little collection job twenty years ago." Conti tapped a finger against his temple. "I don't forget anything."

"Me, neither," J.D. said. "Don't worry. Go on home. I'll be in touch."

Sam felt as if she watched it all through a thick pane of glass, but when Carmen finally turned for the big black SUV at the curb she snapped to attention.

"Carmen," she called out and the blonde paused. "Are you okay?" Frank and J.D.'s eyes both swiveled to her and she fought her fear.

"Jesus Christ, Sam," J.D. muttered. "Shut up."

Sam ignored him. "Do you need help?" she asked and Carmen looked at her hands for a moment and then at her husband.

"I'm fine," she said and walked toward the car.

After a moment, Francis followed his wife. His oily gaze flickered to Sam, taking in her robe and bare feet and Sam had never felt so naked in her life. Nearly defiled.

"Nice cooz," he murmured to J.D. and she felt J.D.'s whole body tense, like he was about to spring. So Sam stepped in front of him, protecting the bastard with her body.

Once their shadows were off her stoop, she stepped back inside, waiting for J.D. to join her.

She slammed the door and whirled on him.

"What the hell do you think you're doing?" she cried.

"My job," he said, turning and heading for the shelter's bedrooms.

"Did you think maybe we should've talked about the

situation before you decided to deliver a pregnant sixteen-year-old girl to her abusive father."

"No," he said, not even looking at her. "I didn't."

"What are you going to do?" she asked, absolutely unable to believe he would hand over that girl to her father.

"What I am being paid to do," he said, crossing the threshold into his room. He tore off his shirt and dug out a clean one from the bag on the bed.

"Please, J.D. You aren't this man. We need to talk. I need to talk to Christina before she goes home. I need to assess if this is the right move."

"It's not really your call," J.D. said. He sat on the bed and tugged on socks, jamming his feet into his boots.

"I don't understand what's happening here," she said, stunned, watching him like he was a movie or something. Something not real. Not connected to her.

"It's pretty simple, Sam. I am doing my job," he barked. "I take jobs and money and in return I do whatever people want me to. I find daughters. I catch cheating wives. I take pictures. Video. I provide all the proof anyone could ever need that people are lying animals."

Sam rocked back for a second, suddenly aware that there were too many things at work. Too many people in the room.

His face scared her. Not that he was angry, or close to violence as he had been earlier.

He was blank. Emotionless.

And that scared her to death.

"Who am I dealing with right now?" she asked, wrapping her arms around her waist. "J.D.? The man who made love to me last night? The man who taught his son how to swing on a rope? Or Jakos Diavoletes? The butcher's son."

"There's only been me," he told her. "The lovemaking and rope swing garbage was a lie."

"What?"

"For ten years, every time I walked into this house, I pretended to be someone I wasn't. Last night. Yesterday. The first time we made love. All of it was fake. None of it was me."

"I don't believe you."

"Don't believe me?" he asked, emotion sparking in his eyes. "What more proof do you need, Sam? I almost beat that man bloody outside your shelter. I would have killed him if I had to."

"You were provoked," she said, shaking her head. He was slipping into someplace dark and she didn't think she could reach him. "You said you would keep me safe," she said. "That's what you were doing."

"Spence was scared of me. He didn't want me to go upstairs with him," he said brutally.

"He's a little boy," she said, knowing how much that must have hurt J.D. "He doesn't know what he saw. He was scared."

"Listen to yourself," he said, his eyes filled with scorn. "Are you that desperate that you'll forgive anything?"

Oh, he was pushing her. Trying to hurt her. Trying to get her to walk away, to throw him out because he thought that's what he deserved.

It was now or never. She felt the past and the future and all possible options for her life converge right here. Right now. Her courage surged inside of her, combined with her love for him. Her respect for all that he survived. All that he was and could be.

"Maybe everything away from me and away from Serenity was the lie," she said. "Maybe the man who made love to me and taught his kid how to swing on a rope and brought me a guard dog is the real you," she whispered and he went still as if he was absorbing every word, and hope surged in her chest.

"I love you," she said.

The moment swelled, filled the room, pushed against her chest, her burning eyes. "I always have and I always will," she said, when he didn't say anything. Finally he looked up at her and her hope floundered. His eyes were unreadable, unfamiliar. His face a closed book. Panic lanced her courage, but she didn't look away. She didn't give up on this moment. On this man.

Please, J.D. See what I am offering you. See what could be.

"He called you my whore," J.D. said.

She knew what he was doing and she couldn't bear it. *Don't do this*, she wanted to cry. *Don't do this to us.*

"Conti, when he left, he actually called you worse than my whore."

"I'm not," she said, her voice shaking, her entire body shaking, knowing that a terrible pain was coming. It was only a matter of moments. Her mouth was dry. Her courage gone and now she was desperate. She was scared and sad and made out of glass that was shattering. "I would be your wife. I would have your kids."

If you'd let me. She couldn't say the words.

J.D. swayed backward, his face for one moment revealing a hurt so profound. But then he righted himself, closed himself off. Sutured that wound.

"I won't be back," he said, turning. He grabbed his duffel bag and breezed past her.

"You aren't this man, J.D. This isn't you!" she cried.

The door slammed.

Sam couldn't breathe for a moment. She collapsed

against the wall, clutching her stomach as pain exploded in every part of her body.

After a moment she heard his car start then drive away. She listened as long and as hard as she could until the silence roared in her ears.

J. D. Kronos was gone.

14

With lead feet and a broken heart, Sam climbed the stairs to her apartment. Spence sat, white-faced and still, on top of his made bed. His little overnight bag at his feet. His notebook on his lap.

"I want to go home," he said. "I want my mom."

Sam's breath broke as more pain sliced through her. Feeling a million years old, she sat down next to him. "She'll be here in two days."

"Can't we call her?" he asked. "Tell her to come and get me?"

Sam blinked back tears. "I suppose we can," she said. "If that's what you really want to do?"

Spence was quiet for a long time and Sam guessed that this was only normal. Natural. That she lost everything all at once was probably better than losing J.D. and then Spence days later. One cataclysmic rip in her life. She could handle that. She could. She was strong. Tough.

Oh, but the hurt was so much bigger than her. So much heavier than she could carry.

"Is J.D. gone?" Spence asked and she nodded, her throat thick.

"Is that scary guy gone?"

"Yes," she said quickly, looking right into his eyes, desperate to assure him. "And he won't be back. Ever."

Spence took a deep breath and looked down at his notebook.

"J.D. was going to hurt that man, wasn't he?"

Sam thought about it and shook her head. "I don't think he would have done it. But he thought he was protecting us, like Daisy."

"J.D. is a guard dog?"

Sam smiled, barely. "Sort of."

"Why did he leave?"

Because he's a coward. Because he's in too much pain. Because he can't see the future I see. "It's complicated," she said.

"Was it because of me?" Spence asked.

"No," Sam lied slightly. "Not at all, Spence."

"I think I hurt his feelings," Spence said, tracing the skateboarder on the notebook with his finger. "I was really scared."

"It's okay," she said. "Everything is going to be okay." Which was such utter nonsense, she doubted he was actually going to be comforted. But then the little boy's head dropped onto her shoulder, a sad weight.

"Do you still want to call your mom?" she asked, pressing her cheek to the top of his silky hair, unable to stop the tears that ran down her cheeks.

"Not right now," he whispered and he settled in a little better against her shoulder.

Daisy flopped down across their feet and nobody moved.

Not for a very long time.

THE NEXT MORNING Sam and Spence were ghosts. They sat at tables. Walked through rooms. Talked to people as if they were there, but they weren't really. Sam held up her hand and wondered why she couldn't see through it.

"Sam?" Deb asked, coming up behind her as Sam stared out the front picture window, her coffee growing cold. "You all right?"

"Sure," she said, with no conviction. The sky was the color of J.D.'s eyes and she couldn't look away. Couldn't blink in fear that it might change and she'd never see that color again.

"You've got that nutrition class in about twenty minutes."

Sam nodded and without turning to Deb she did something she hadn't done in years. "I am going to need some time off," she said.

"When?" Deb asked, her hand a warm weight on Sam's shoulder. She liked Deb for a lot of reasons, but she loved her right now for not asking about J.D.

"Right now," she said, blinking back tears. "I just can't..." ...*do anything*, she thought. *I can barely stand here.*

"No problem," Deb said, right away. "I can cover your classes."

Sam nodded, feeling the boundaries of her world fall down. Shake loose. Everything that had been right in her world before—living here, working here, never, ever leaving here—all seemed so terribly wrong. Sick even.

"Do you want my apartment?" Sam asked, watching a plastic bag blow down the street. "I'm moving out."

"What? Why?" Deb asked. "You live here."

"Ten years is long enough," she said.

"You quitting the shelter?" Deb asked.

"I can still be the director and not live here," Sam said, not exactly sure how to do that, but she could figure it out. She had to, because she couldn't live like this anymore. "I think it would be better for me."

"Amen to that," Deb said.

"So do you want the apartment?"

"Hell, no." Deb shook her head, laughing. "I believe in life-work balance," she said and Sam felt her ears burn.

Life-work balance was something she hadn't had in ten years. She wasn't even sure what that would be like.

"You know, it's not like we've got women beating down our doors to stay here. Juny and Sue stayed for months because there was no one coming to take their place. In the past two years we've had about six women stay here. Maybe we can use the rooms to teach a few more classes since we're running those at about capacity," Deb suggested. "And if women do show up needing a place to stay we can work something out."

Sam nodded, too wrung out to think of ideas now.

"We can figure it out later," Deb said, giving Sam's shoulder a squeeze before leaving.

She saw Spence's reflection in the window as he stepped into the doorway from the kitchen.

"You want to go swimming?" she asked and his reflection smiled, wide and bright.

IT WAS STUPIDLY easy to find Christina and her boyfriend. Brett Trachten used his father's stolen credit card to get a room at the Tides Motor Lodge outside of Virginia Beach.

After some minor computer hacking J.D. was on his way to the coast.

Four hours and one quick call to Greg later he stood in front of the dented aluminum door of room twelve at one of the dingiest roadside motels he'd ever seen. And he'd seen a lot.

Looking at the waterless swimming pool that someone was trying to fill with crushed Budweiser cans, he was glad Sam wasn't here to see this. It would break her heart to see where Christina had run to.

He stared up at the unrelenting midafternoon sun and tried not to wonder what Sam and Spence were doing right now.

What he would be doing if he was with them.

He pounded his fist against the door and listened to the frantic murmured voices inside the room and the scuffle and thump of someone tripping on their way out of bed.

God save me from stupid kids.

"Christina. Brett," he said, looking into the peephole, directly, he was sure, into the eyeball of one Brett Trachten. "Open up."

More scuffling. More voices. Finally, the door cracked and Christina's face poked out under the chain. "What are you doing here, J.D.?"

Her efforts at coolness were slightly heartbreaking, here among the ruins of the Tides Motel.

"Taking in the sights," he said sardonically. "You've got a lot of people worried about you."

"I left Sam a note and—"

Just hearing her name was a searing pain behind his eyes. "Your parents came looking for you," he interrupted out of self-preservation.

That got the girl's attention. Her eyes went wide and she ducked back, shutting the door while she undid the chain. She stepped out of the shadowed room. "It's okay, Brett," she said, over her shoulder. In the heat and away from the shelter, she managed to look a little tougher. A little harder, as though the decisions she was making were already having an effect.

The baggy Killers concert T-shirt she wore only made her look more pregnant, and younger.

The combination was scary and he wanted to pick her up and take her out of here, back where Sam could take care of her.

"They were at the shelter?" she asked.

He nodded.

Christina licked her lips, picked at the crumbling paint on the doorway. "My dad?"

Even miles away from the man she was scared, he could see it in the tense corners of her mouth, the way she put a hand over her belly.

"He was there," was all he said and she still went pale.

Christina sighed and pushed her fingers through her chin-length hair, piling it up on her head, revealing blond roots from her sloppy dye job. Glancing back at the door then back at J.D., she seemed to be coming to a decision.

"You're here to take me back to the Serenity House?"

He shook his head. He'd been thinking a lot about what kind of man he was. He'd been thinking about it until his head ached and his body felt like cement and his heart stopped beating in his chest. He'd never be Sam's man. But he couldn't be the man he was before, either.

J.D. had felt this crossroads coming. Even as he left Serenity, the diamond ring burning a hole in his pocket, he'd known this moment would happen.

The old J.D. wouldn't even be standing here talking to her. He'd have her in the car, bound and gagged if he had to. To hell with what she wanted.

But the man who spent the past weekend with Spencer... With Sam. Christina. He couldn't do it.

"I'm here to give you a choice," he said.

"She won't go back to her folks." Brett, a strong, tall kid who looked older than seventeen, stepped out of the room. He measured J.D. from head to foot and glared at him. The kid meant business. "It's not safe. Not for her. Not for the baby."

"Or you," Christina said, watching him with wide eyes.

The emotion between these two was thick and the pregnancy and on-the-run situation they were in pushed it past the standard teenager variety.

Brett reached out and stroked her hair, cupping a hand around her neck.

"You can't stay here, Christina," J.D. told her, interrupting the teenage lovefest with a little dose of the tough reality they were currently floundering in. Christina glanced around, taking in the motel's chipping paint and cracked asphalt in the parking lot.

"It seemed kind of romantic last night," she whispered, a blush on her cheeks.

"Sure, I can see that," he said, watching a seagull peck at a cigarette butt.

"I'll go back to the shelter," she said firmly, but clearly reluctant to leave Brett.

"You can't go back to Serenity," he told her. There was no way he was putting Sam back in the path of Frank Conti again.

"Then we'll just keep moving," Brett said, his arm around her. His chin came up, like he was ready to fight for his girl and the baby. While J.D. could respect the intention, it was a bit stupid considering their situation.

"Your father's credit card has been reported stolen," J.D.

told them, bursting their bubble, but not confessing to having done the reporting. "So, unless you have some other way to get money, you won't get far."

"I shouldn't have given Sam my ring," she whispered to Brett, her distress clearly growing. J.D. knew they could feel the walls closing in on them, because he had designed them to do that. "We could have hocked it."

J.D. tugged the ring free from his pocket and handed it to them. "It's a nice ring, but it still won't get you far."

"Well, I'm not going back to my parents," she nearly cried, her cheeks going red with sudden anger. She grabbed the ring out of his hand. "This will just have to work for a while."

"There's another way," he said, looking at Brett and seeing the knowledge in his eyes.

"What?" Tina looked back at Brett. "What's he talking about?"

"A guy from the FBI talked to me a few days ago," Brett said, stroking her hair, reaching for her when she pulled away, shaking her head.

"About what?"

"That run I took for your dad up to New York City," he said. "The thing with the cigarettes." His eyes flickered over to J.D., and he saw something in them. Something dark and scared and older than his years. "And the guy."

"Oh, my God." She started breathing hard. "Oh, my God, you were going to rat out my dad."

"Do you blame me?" he asked. "He was going to kill me when we told your folks we were pregnant."

"But now he will for sure," she cried, tugging on his arm. "We've got to go."

"I didn't talk to them," he said. "This agent wanted me to

go into a protection program and I couldn't do that without you so I ran."

"That agent is a friend of mine," J.D. said. "And the offer still stands. Whatever you know about your father's business activities and in return they can promise you complete protection."

"Right," she cried, her eyes wild. "Like that's possible."

"It is," he said. "They can take care of you. They can take care of your child."

She put her face in her hands and J.D. wished Sam was here to say the right thing. To comfort her, because J.D. didn't know how to do it.

"You should at least talk to my friend," he told her. "Hear him out."

Brett and Tina looked at each other for a long time, saying nothing, but communicating all the same. He watched them and thought of Sam at the pond the other day. The way she'd looked at all of them with love and bewilderment in her eyes, as if she didn't know how they all came to be together. He thought of that and how he'd known exactly what she was thinking, just by the way she tilted her head.

"You need to be going to the doctor's and taking vitamins," Brett said, snapping J.D. out of his useless memories. "I mean, you are really pregnant and if something happened —" He shook his head, his face white. "I'm so scared. And if they can help...?" His expression was pleading and finally Christina launched herself at Brett, nearly knocking him over with her belly.

"Call him," Brett said, over her shoulder, before burying his head in Tina's hair.

~

THAT NIGHT J.D. lay in his bed, stared up at his ceiling and tried to control himself. He watched the lights of passing cars outside his apartment showcase the bone-white ceiling, the empty room. He could hear the Perisons downstairs screaming, and he thought briefly of the quiet at Serenity House. The thick, palpable quiet.

The way it would wrap around him, soak into him. Insulate him from anything outside of Serenity House.

The phone on his bare chest weighed a thousand pounds and with every breath he felt the weight press harder into his rib cage, until it seemed easier to just not breathe.

Quickly, as fast as he possibly could, as if it were a snake ready to strike, he grabbed the phone, opened it and dialed Sam's phone number.

"J.D.?" Her voice sliced through him like shrapnel and he closed his eyes. "What's—"

"Christina is fine," he said.

"What do you mean?" she asked. "Is she home? What—"

"She's safe," he said, then hung up.

A sadness so painful it felt like anger flooded him and he sat up, hurling the phone against the wall.

"It's over," he said, breathing hard. "Over."

And then he yelled it.

15

Sam looked at Spence and tried to see him as Jennifer would see him. He was clean. That was good. His shirt wasn't too wrinkled. His hair was combed. He had a sunburn across the top of his nose and cheeks from their two days spent at the pond.

Sam thought it made the kid look healthy.

Jennifer would probably take him to the hospital upon seeing it.

But the best part was the notebook that had been attached to his side was upstairs in his backpack. He hadn't carried it around at all yesterday and today it didn't even come down for breakfast.

"You excited?" she asked him needlessly. Spence didn't even turn away from his lookout at the front window.

"Yep," he said, scanning left and right for Jennifer's silver Jetta.

Sam stepped up beside him and brushed her fingers through his hair, messing it up a little, but she was unable to resist.

He was leaving.

And she didn't really know what that meant.

"I had a lot of fun with you," she said, watching him watch for his mother. The excitement in his eyes was a little like sandpaper against her heart, but she couldn't look away.

"Me, too," he said. "I had a lot of fun." He glanced up at her. "Most of the time."

Right, she thought. About that...

"Maybe we shouldn't bring up that scary guy. Or J.D."

He shot her a look like she was the dumbest person on the planet. "Duh," he said. "My mom would have a heart attack."

Sam tried not to laugh, but couldn't help it. Man, she was going to miss Spence.

"There she is!" he cried, jumping up at the sight of a car turning down the road.

"Well." Sam squinted. "I don't know—"

"It's her. I know it." Spence was out the door and running across the front yard to the sidewalk, just as the car became distinguishable as a silver Jetta.

Well, Sam thought, a bittersweet sadness creeping up on her. *What do you know.*

The car was barely stopped before Jennifer was hurtling herself out the driver's side door and into the lawn where she fell on her knees and crushed Spence to her.

It was simply too much. J.D. leaving. And now Spence. Sam's heart, as if set in icy water for too long, stopped feeling the pain and went numb. Her whole body went numb as if shutting down a little, to protect itself from harm.

Sam watched them, knowing she should probably give them some privacy, but she didn't know if she'd ever see Spence again. And so, looking away, even for a moment for all the right reasons, was impossible.

Jennifer cupped Spence's face in her hands, running her

thumbs over the sunburn, as if she could erase it and Sam winced. She was talking to Spence, very seriously, and after a second Spence's arms flew up into the air.

Jennifer seemed surprised but then thrilled, pulling her son to her and rocking him gently against her.

Sam's numb heart couldn't withstand that and she finally had to turn away.

She went to the kitchen and tried to be happy for Spence and Jennifer.

A few minutes later, the front door opened with a bang and she whirled to see Spence charging into the kitchen like a boy on fire.

"Guess what, Sam?" he cried.

"Wha—"

"We're going to stay."

Sam braced herself against the counter, too stunned to speak.

"For a few days," Jennifer clarified, coming to stand behind Spence. "And only if it's okay."

Jennifer looked different. Good. Some of the pinched misery around her mouth and in her eyes was gone and, while sadness still surrounded her like a coat, she didn't seem quite so brittle. So desperate.

Sam struggled to flip her mind around to actually say something and she must have been gaping like a fish, because finally Jennifer cupped Spence's shoulder.

"Sweetheart," she said. "Can you give Sam and I a second?"

"Sure," he said. "I'll go get your suitcase."

Once Spence was gone, Jennifer approached Sam. "Are you all right?"

"I'm..." ...*totally falling apart.* "Confused. What's... ah... what's going on?"

"I quit my job," Jennifer said as if she were saying the sun was out. "I interviewed the First Lady and driving back to Baltimore I realized that if I had to spend one more night in a house that smelled like Doug I would—" she took a deep breath "—lose it. Just come totally undone. And then I realized that it wasn't just the house. It was my life. Without Doug I don't want that life. I don't want to try to slip back into it without him."

"So you quit your job?"

"I quit my job."

Sam blinked, trying to reconcile this woman with the woman who left here and she couldn't do it.

"And you're staying...here?"

"For a few days, until a house I rented in Asheville for the summer can be made ready."

"Asheville." Sam nodded. She felt a strange jealousy for the strength Jennifer had. It was as if they'd switched places and Jennifer was the one on solid ground, while Sam was getting cozy at rock bottom. "Spence will like that."

"He'll like staying here for a few days better," Jennifer said with a twinkle in her eye that Sam never would have been able to guess was possible.

She's not taking Spence away.

"Me, too," Sam said, trying not to cry, but her breath caught on a big heavy sob. Her body was splintering, breaking apart like a boat against a shore and she couldn't stop it. She couldn't control herself.

"Whoa, whoa," Jennifer said, coming forward to gingerly touch Sam's shoulder as though the grief might spread by contact. "Are you okay?" she asked. "Are you—"

"No," Sam admitted. "I'm not."

And then, the biggest surprise of all, Jennifer hugged her. She just leaned in past the tears and pulled Sam close.

"It's going to be okay," Jennifer said. "Whatever's wrong, it will be okay."

No, it won't, Sam thought. *It won't ever be okay.*

J.D. SAT beside Greg at the dark corner table in the bar off the Beltway.

"Christ, man," Greg bitched. "I was about to leave."

"Sorry," J.D. said, without really meaning it. He shrugged out of his coat and settled back into the wooden seat.

He'd been lying low for three months, ever since Greg took Christina and Brett into custody. He wasn't sure if Conti and his crew would put two and two together and get J.D., so he put his head down just in case.

But now that Francis Conti's arrest had been made, his bail set at about a gazillion dollars, J.D. figured he could poke his head up for one quick drink.

"You all right?" Greg asked, drinking the last of the beer in front of him, then wiping his mustache with a his giant paw. "'Cause you look like shit."

J.D. ignored him, focused instead on the blond waitress walking toward him. She gave him a quick once-over with her hard eyes and he apparently passed some test because her walk got a little looser. As though her hips were suddenly greased.

J.D. wanted to be turned on by her. By the utter ease of it all. The anonymity of it. He didn't know her, or care about her or spend nights thinking about her. He could screw her, scratch this itch that was killing him, then he could get on with his life.

Something he hadn't been able to do in ten years. But she left him cold.

Instead, stupidly, what seemed more appealing was driving down to Northwoods and parking down the street from Serenity and waiting to catch a glimpse of Sam.

Sooner or later the urge was going to get too strong to fight and he'd be on the highway like some sick stalker.

Oh, the things I have to look forward to, he thought bitterly.

"Two beers," he said, cutting off the blonde's smile before it had a chance to really get going. "And a burger. Put it on his tab," he said, jerking a thumb at Greg.

"Wonderful," Greg said when the waitress stalked off. "You're an hour late and I still have to pay."

J.D. didn't say anything and Greg leaned forward, trying to look at his face in the smoky darkness of the bar they met in once every few months. "You all right?"

No. He wasn't. He was bleeding from some wound he couldn't find.

"Fine," he said. "Congrats on the arrest," he said, changing the subject.

"Thank you," Greg said and took the two beers the waitress brought over. "Thank you very much. I think with the info the kids gave us we should be able to make this stick."

J.D. tried not to ask. Tried not to care, but he couldn't seem to stop himself. "How are the kids?"

"Good," Greg said. "She had the baby. A boy. Everybody's healthy."

Something in J.D. soared. Something he was totally unaware existed inside of him.

"They gave him up for adoption," Greg said and J.D. paused while lifting his glass to his lips.

Amazing, he thought and then just as quickly he thought of Sam and how much she would want to know.

He thought of Sam's face hearing that news. Her smile.

Her tears. The bright light that shot out of her when she was happy.

She should know about that baby.

And suddenly, like the information pried open a door he'd locked and forgotten about, he realized everything she didn't know.

She doesn't know I love her, he thought. *She doesn't know I can't sleep at night. That I can't taste air or water without thinking of how she tasted. She doesn't know that I've been more dead than alive for the past three months.*

"J.D.?" Greg asked, clapping a heavy hand on his shoulder. "You all right?"

J.D. stood, pulled a twenty from his pocket and tossed it on the table. "No," he said. "But maybe I will be."

THE SOUND of air brakes snapped J.D. awake from the coma he'd been in.

He jerked upright, banging his chest against the steering wheel. His elbow against the driver's side door.

"Oh, man," he muttered, rubbing his elbow and trying to roll out the kinks in his shoulders and lower back. Sleeping in his car. Had he really come to this?

The news about the baby and the adoption had put him on the road to Sam. Imagining her face when he told her had given him the reason he'd been waiting a month for.

A reason to sleep in his car outside Serenity House.

A reason to see her.

A reason to talk to her.

A reason to live again.

The sun had risen, and the front lawn of Serenity House

seemed a little foreign. Surreal. Because of all the boxes. And the movers.

And the way Sam stood amongst it all like a redheaded Napoleon.

Last night the house had been still, the lawn empty.

Now, it was the scene of a move.

Warm Carolina air blew through his open window, carrying her voice, her laughter as she joked around with one of the guys. Through the windshield of his car she was a vision of every single thing he thought he never truly deserved and he realized how stupid it was to be here. To have driven all night to tell her something he could have e-mailed her.

Was she leaving? Was it too late? It was the only answer.

He put his head down on the steering wheel.

"Idiot," he muttered, thumping his forehead against the leather. "Such. An. Idiot."

He leaned back, pressing his arms straight, gripping the wheel and looked up. Right into Sam's eyes. She'd seen him. Amongst the mayhem in her yard she'd found him.

As he watched, her hand fell to her side. Paper fluttered from her fingers.

He felt their connection like electricity in the air. Everyone, everything, every sight and sound vanished and for a perfect moment it was just them. Him and Sam.

Like it used to be. Like it should have been all along.

If this connection was here, she had to feel something. Even hatred. He could deal with hatred. He was so damn glad he hadn't killed everything she'd felt for him.

On autopilot, guided by something outside of himself, something so big and all-consuming he was powerless against it, he opened the door.

His love for Sam was his compass. His engine. And he

got out of the car and crossed the lawn. He wanted to run to her, relieved to see her again, happy that he'd mustered up this courage. But as he got closer he realized that it was anger he saw in her eyes. A whole lot of it.

"What are you doing here?" she said. Her tone indicated she'd prefer him someplace else. Like Mars.

"I wanted to talk to you," he whispered, moving sideways as movers carrying Sam's bed came down the stairs. "What's going on here?"

"I'm moving." She crossed her arms over her chest and her chin was up, so defiant and strong, and he nearly evaporated with his love for her and his fear that he'd lost her.

"Away?" he asked, stunned that she would leave the shelter.

"To town."

"What about the shelter?"

"I can run the shelter and not live here. What do you want, J.D.?"

He looked at her, watched her, opened his heart, felt himself waver, thin and diminish. He was water. Then air. He was nothing. He let it all go. The things he'd done. The things he'd seen. And he concentrated on her and rebuilt himself. Piece by piece into the man he was when he was with her. The man he wanted to be.

"My..." He licked his lips. "My name is J. D. Kronos," he said and her eyelids flinched. "I used to be a private investigator, but I quit. I'm not sure what I am doing now. Not that that would be a problem. I like to work." He paused. "I live in Newark in my uncle Milo's old condo. It's a dump and I don't feel like it's my home. I never have. Once a year I send my sister a thousand dollars, but she doesn't know who it's from. I'm a good cook, my uncle taught me. I like football."

He was rambling. Really running in circles, so he decided to get right to the point. He took a deep breath.

"And I love you. I know I'm not what you want or need." Oh, God, wasn't that the truth? Just saying the words to her silent, impassive face proved what a fool he was for trying this. But he couldn't quite get himself to shut up. "But I wanted you to know that. To know that the man I am when I am with you is the man I want to be. The man..."

She wasn't responding. She just stood there, breathing hard, her eyes not blinking. "I..." He took a deep breath. This didn't work. It was a waste of time, he was too late. "I just wanted to say that." He stepped backward, lifting his hand, wanting so badly to touch her, but just saying goodbye. "Take care, Sam."

She grabbed his hand. Her palm was sweaty, her grip strong. His fingers curled around hers instinctively. Like she was a rope from shore and he was a drowning man.

"My name is Sam Riggins," she whispered. "I work too much but I am trying to fix that. I bought a house. A little one in town. With a bedroom for Spence when he comes and visits. I am trying to work on myself. On lots of things. I'm trying to find hobbies, but I hate knitting. I'm a terrible cook." She smiled and he realized that tears had gathered in her eyes. He was suddenly weightless. Off the ground. Only her hand kept him in place. "And I love you. I've always loved you and you are exactly what I need. You are what I have always wanted."

She tugged on his hand, because he was still too stunned to act, and then he was in her arms, held tight by her strength. Breathing in her perfect rose smell.

Sam. His whole body sighed like a weary traveler arriving home. And suddenly the fog cleared. It was Sam in his arms. Sam crying. Sam holding him so hard he hurt. It was always Sam.

Holy crap, he thought, wanting to laugh and bawl at the same time. It worked.

"I thought I was too late," he whispered into the crook of her neck, his lips on her skin, her hair under his fingers. The many smells and textures of this woman bringing him back to life.

"You're just in time," she whispered back.

EPILOGUE

J.D. had a home. His first real one. Filled with furniture that matched and books and CDs and the woman he loved. She made him coffee every morning and he made her dinner every night and sometimes they talked about the past and sometimes they didn't talk at all.

He was renovating each room, stripping the floors, painting the walls, putting his blood, sweat and tears into a little bungalow that a month ago he'd never seen, and now he was mad for. Sick over.

She joked sometimes that he loved the house more than her and he always felt compelled to show her otherwise.

He couldn't love anything more than he loved her.

He'd even managed to take control of his job. He was still a P.I., but he no longer took the jobs that made him ill. No more cheating spouses, no more workers' comp or insurance fraud.

"J.D.?" Sam whispered, wrapping her arms around his waist from behind him. Her hands slipped up his chest, over his pounding heart. "Honey? Are you okay?" Her fingers flew down to his wrist, taking his pulse and he reversed their grip, bringing her fingers to his mouth.

"I'm nervous," he admitted. "Last time I saw the kid he was so scared of me he didn't want me around him."

"He felt so bad about that," she said, turning him away from the front bay window, where he'd been standing guard waiting for a sign of a silver Jetta.

"He shouldn't." J.D. laughed in a rough burst. "He was right to be scared of me." God, he was so nervous he was practically sick with it. Spence and Jennifer were coming through Northwoods on their way back to Baltimore after the summer in Asheville and he felt like he was about to face a firing squad. He was terrified of what the boy might do. How he might react to him.

So help him, if the boy was scared of him, J.D. didn't think he could take it.

"It will be fine," Sam whispered. "You'll see."

J.D. still had his doubts, his lingering distrust that things would be fine for him, but he didn't like to argue with Sam. Instead, he wrapped his arms around her and hoped that she was right.

"They're here," Sam said and he whirled to face the window. Sure enough, a silver Jetta was there.

J.D. opened the front door and stepped out into the yard just as the car's back door opened and a little redheaded boy with J.D.'s eyes and Sam's hair tumbled out. A boy with a sunburn and freckles that hadn't been there in June.

"J.D.!" Spence cried, joy lighting up his face.

And then the boy was running and so was J.D.

J.D. crouched down and then fell onto his knees in the grass just as the little boy hit him, his body a heavy pencil-scented missile.

"I missed you, J.D.," Spence whispered in his ear.

"Not as much as I missed you," J.D. assured him. Spence's arms wrapped around his neck and J.D. closed his eyes, relief an animal he could no longer contain.

Wrapping his arms around Spence's back, he thanked God for Sam. For this boy and the long road that brought them all together.

THANK you SO MUCH for reading Sam and J.D's story. I hope you enjoyed it!

Please join my newsletter list or my facebook group The Keepers where I share all my news and do tons of giveaways and author visits!

JENNIFER AND SPENCER get their own story in AND THEN THERE WAS YOU which is available NOW!

THE SCOOP of Jennifer Stern's career has just landed on her doorstep. Literally. Ian Greer—the playboy millionaire—is everything the headlines claim. Charming, flirtatious, and ready for a good time. But Jennifer soon suspects he's pulling a fast one and there's a different man behind the handsome mask he shows the world. He's a puzzle she longs to unravel.

TOO BAD SHE'S turned her back on that part of her life. No longer a journalist Jennifer just longs to be with her son and heal from the last few years of her life. Years that nearly killed her.

. . .

Soon she find it impossible to resist the story. And even more impossible to resist the man. But if she breaks the story, will she lose the man?

CHAPTER ONE

Jennifer Stern was a logical, sensible woman. And, she told herself, logical, sensible women didn't stand on chairs, screaming.

No matter how much they wanted to.

"Do you see it?" Deb Barber asked, from her position on one of the chairs.

"I can't see anything," Jennifer said, her own logical, sensible, stupid feet firmly planted on the floor. She had to yell in order to be heard over the cacophony of spraying water.

A geyser licked across the ceiling from the broken faucet then splashed onto the floor, creating a lake in the middle of the kitchen.

And while she couldn't see the snake, she knew it was somewhere between her and the water shut-off valve.

"It's just a garter snake," she said, inching around the fridge. "Right?" This is why she lived in cities. Cities with plumbers. Cities that didn't have snakes just roaming through kitchens.

"I have no idea," Deb answered, crouching and resting her hot pink wrist-casts on the back of the wooden chair. "All I know is it was big. A big snake in the middle of the kitchen."

Jennifer ducked under the geyser and stepped gingerly over the lake, with one eye out for visiting reptiles.

When she'd agreed to help out for two weeks at Serenity House while her friends Samantha and J.D. went on a much-needed vacation she had not agreed to this.

"Tell me if you see it," Jennifer said, feeling vulnerable as she ducked under the counter and cranked off the water supply.

It was probably just a garter snake. Or, even more likely, a figment of Deb's imagination.

"I didn't make it up," Deb said, her voice loud in the sudden quiet. "I swear I saw a snake."

"I never said you didn't," Jennifer said quickly, wondering if Deb wasn't just a little psychic. She wouldn't be all that surprised. If Deb could sprout wings and fly, Jennifer wouldn't even blink.

Officially, Deb was in charge of Serenity since Sam and J.D. left. But a bad fall resulting in two broken wrists made doing anything required in the day-to-day running of a small community center pretty much impossible.

Which is why Jennifer was here. Deb was the brains, Jennifer was the wrists.

"Hey, wow, Mom, look."

At the sound of her son Spencer's voice, she jumped and smacked her head scrambling out from under the sink. "Spence, be careful there's a—"

Her eleven-year-old son, red curls catching the late afternoon sun, stood in the doorway to the kitchen holding a small, twisting green snake.

"Oh, dear lord," Deb breathed. "Honey, you need to put that thing down."

"Why?" Spence asked, glancing at Deb. "It's just a garter."

Daisy, Serenity's giant guard dog and Spence's constant

companion when he was at the shelter, barked once as if to second that assessment.

"You're not scared of a garter, are you, Daisy?" Spence asked, dangling the snake over the half-rottweiler, half-whatever-lived-under-the-Munsters'-stairs beast. Daisy's tail didn't even twitch.

Jennifer collapsed against the counter because her knees were gone. And because she was so glad her son was a young biologist and knew he wasn't holding a cottonmouth, and because Deb looked absolutely ridiculous on the kitchen chair with her hot pink wrist-casts and ebony dreadlocks, Jennifer did something she hadn't done in ages. She laughed.

She laughed so hard she wiped her eyes.

She laughed so hard she kind of had to go to the bathroom.

"Mom?" Spence's blue-grey eyes were wide with wonder and a little fear. It had been so long, she realized, so long since he'd seen her happy like this. So long that uncontrolled laughter was scary. *Oh, Spence*, she thought, a sadness gripping her so hard it hurt, *have I been that grim*? "You all right?"

"I'm fine, honey," she reassured him quickly. "Deb thought it was a giant king cobra coming to eat all of us."

Spence's serious face cracked open and his laughter, not as rare as hers but sweet all the same, spilled over the kitchen and made her laugh harder until they were gripping their knees to stay upright.

"Jennifer? Spence?" Deb asked, looking at her as if she'd grown two heads. "You having some kind of fit?"

"Stop it," Jennifer cried.

"I mean, if it was someone else, I'd think you were

laughing. But since in the whole year I've known you I've never seen you so much as giggle—"

"I laugh," she protested. "Spence? Don't I laugh?"

"Not like this you don't."

There hadn't been anything worth laughing about. Not in years. In fact, at some point two years ago, she'd been fairly convinced she'd never laugh again. Never feel joy again.

But here it was. Different than before, harder, sharper, almost painful. But everything was different than before.

Her. Spencer. Life.

But laughing again felt good. Like sex.

Though she was not counting on its return anytime soon.

"I'm going to take the snake outside," Spence said and was out the front door in flash, the screen slamming home behind him and Daisy.

A humid Carolina breeze trickled through that screen, making everything just a little stickier.

"When's the air conditioner going to be fixed?" Jennifer asked. Had she known there were going to be snakes, broken faucets and no air conditioner she definitely would have said no—no matter how much she loved Sam and J.D.

"Gary said it would take him a few hours, when he got here. Should be cool by tomorrow."

"Thank God." She sighed and took in the broken faucet, the giant lake and the water-splashed ceiling, and wondered where to start the clean-up efforts. She'd been here two days and already she had to wonder how Sam did this every day. It seemed like all she and Deb were doing was putting out fires. Snakes. Broken pipes. Hungry kids. Nutrition classes. Parenting classes. Book groups.

Deb ducked into the community center office/supply

closet, tried to grab two big mops and ended up knocking both of them to the ground.

"Stupid casts," she muttered.

"Hey, I'm supposed to be doing that stuff," Jennifer said, and rushed in to get the mops and a big stack of towels. Being incapacitated wasn't easy on anyone but it was particularly rough on Deb, who was used to doing on her own since she ran away from home and right to Serenity House four years ago.

Deb was far, far older than her twenty-two years.

"What do you think about the pipes?" Jennifer asked, laying the white and green towels across the big puddle.

"Even if my wrists weren't busted," Deb said, "I wouldn't be able to fix that faucet. Sam's been holding those pipes together with string and hope for too long now."

"Figures it would fall apart when she was gone."

"Well—" Deb arched a plucked black eyebrow "— maybe with her gone we can actually get them fixed. Serenity House has a private benefactor who as far as I am concerned, doesn't do nearly enough benefacting."

Jennifer paused while mopping. "You're not suggesting we call—" dramatically, she looked left then right "—the mysterious number?" she whispered. When Sam left she'd given Deb and Jennifer this phone number that was only to be used in the case of extreme financial or legal disaster. At the time Jennifer had thought Sam was joking, but J.D. quickly shook his head, indicating the number wasn't something Sam joked about.

Deb tried to look stern, imitating Sam. "We don't make fun of the number."

"Has she ever called the number?" Jennifer asked.

"A few times." Deb kicked a towel over one part of the lake. "Once when there were some legal issues after that estranged husband broke in to the shelter and kidnapped his wife and child. And then other times when she wanted to build the classrooms onto the shelter and get computers. When the roof caved in." She shrugged. "That's it."

"Did the benefactor give you the money?"

"Right away," Deb said, like she couldn't believe it. "It was like he was waiting around for the chance to send money. Sam left a message and within two hours a banker was on the phone wondering where to wire the money."

"Wow."

"Right, wow." Deb was getting worked up. "And when we called with those legal problems, a lawyer contacted us right away and the whole thing just disappeared."

"Does she know who this benefactor is?"

"No idea."

And that, Jennifer thought, was the really wild thing about it. Money just arrived. Legal trouble got fixed. No obligations. No thank-you notes. Nothing. Like magic Sam called this number, left a message and her troubles vanished.

Who wouldn't call that number?

What Jennifer would have done for a number like that two years ago.

Though, she thought with the stabbing pain that had only gotten bearable in the past year, money wouldn't have saved her husband.

She heaved an armful of wet towels into the sink and turned around to look at Deb.

"Do we call this magic number?" she asked.

Deb sighed. "Not yet. Things need to get a lot worse."

BUY And Then There Was You now!

. . .

AND CHECK out the first book in The Riverview Inn series
Wedding At The Riverview Inn

AN EMOTIONAL TALE of a magical inn, a wedding gone terribly wrong and a woman searching for a second chance.

ALICE HAS HIT ROCK BOTTOM. Once a Michelin-starred chef, she is now drowning in debt, working the line at a chain restaurant and drinking too much. The last person she ever expected to come knocking with a job offer and a fresh start is her ex-husband, Gabe.

GABE BUILT The Riverview Inn with his dad and brother. Now, the grand lodge in the Catskill Mountains is nearly ready for the opening event—a society wedding for 500 guests.

THE ONLY THING missing is a chef. That's where Alice comes in.

THE DEAL GABE offers Alice is too good to pass up: help him get through this wedding and he'll get her out of debt.

BUT NOTHING IS simple at The Riverview and soon she's dealing with a bridezilla, pink swans, a series of mysterious letters and a teenage delinquent. Through it all, one thing is clear—her feelings for Gabe burn as bright as they always have.

When the wedding is over, will Alice walk away for good? Or will The Riverview work its magic on Alice and Gabe?

THE RIVERVIEW INN SERIES

Three books, three women who find the unexpected at a gorgeous Inn nestled in the Catskill Mountains.
    Wedding At The Riverview Inn
    Secrets of The Riverview Inn
    Home to The Riverview Inn

An emotional tale of a magical inn, a wedding gone terribly wrong and a woman searching for a second chance.

Alice has hit rock bottom. Once a Michelin-starred chef, she is now drowning in debt, working the line at a chain restaurant and drinking too much. The last person she ever expected to come knocking with a job offer and a fresh start is her ex-husband, Gabe.

Gabe built The Riverview Inn with his dad and brother. Now, the grand lodge in the Catskill Mountains is nearly ready for the opening event—a society wedding for 500 guests.

The only thing missing is a chef. That's where Alice comes in.

The deal Gabe offers Alice is too good to pass up: help him get through this wedding and he'll get her out of debt.

But nothing is simple at The Riverview and soon she's dealing with a bridezilla, pink swans, a series of mysterious letters and a teenage delinquent. Through it all, one thing is clear—her feelings for Gabe burn as bright as they always have.

When the wedding is over, will Alice walk away for good? Or will The Riverview work its magic on Alice and Gabe?

Made in the USA
Monee, IL
22 August 2021

76226016R00128